Glittery Literary

A collection of sparḳ ⌐f our winning
entries and other careft ⌐ly recommended

Colin,

Something for your
retirement!

All the best

Lee

GLITTERY LITERARY

OUR LONG TERM GOALS:

To elevate great writers by providing a platform for their work.

To help reduce child poverty by donating profit to a selection of charities.

Thank you to all of the wonderful contributors whose work features in this booklet and to everybody that entered.

JOIN US IN OUR BEAUTIFUL PROJECT.

www.glitteryliterary.com

glitteryliterary@gmail.com

APRIL 2021 CONTENTS

Lustrous Longs:

Two Rings by Lee Greenaway (Winner)

The Pull of the Tides by Roz Levens (Second Place)

When You're Chosen, You're Chosen by Daniel Marques

She Bleeds with the Fields by Gracious Love

Sailboat by Jarrett Mazza

Lord of the Feathers by Steve Goodlad

Moustachio by Laura Scotland

My Girlfriend's Plants by Robert Scott

Private View by Steve Gregory

4.9 Stars by Joe Howsin

Mrs. Bowley Upstairs by Ed Walsh

Passing Ships by Rosie Cullen

The Weathermen—A Love Letter by Aneeta Sundararaj

The Shadow Waved Back by Leena Batchelor

Passing On by Polly Palmer

Evensong by John Hargreaves

A Contained Life by Rebecca Kinnarney

The Right Place by Sven Camrath

Someone, No-one by Hilary Coyne

The Chair by Miki Lentin

As Cold as a Winter's Day by Derek Hulme

The Displacement Artist by David DeWinter

SHIMMERING SHORTS

Attraversiamo by Kerry Rawlinson (Winner)

The Coloureds (Maria's label) occupied next-door's weed-rotted clapboard last spring. We seldom saw them. *Good thing,* Maria opined. Life on the knife-edge of nothing, I thought—but said nothing. It never paid to contradict Maria. She bought window blinds and closed them. *I don't need to watch the neighbourhood deteriorate.* She didn't, in the end. She left.

This winter's been particularly vicious. In the old days, the neighbourhood was *classier, more respectable.* Winter dressed the world in Christmas loveliness, with picturesque snowscapes for jovial Santas, Rudolphs with flashing noses, trios of Wise Men. Festive wreaths graced front doors, and the season rang with kids' laughter.

Since the factory opened, it's an alien world. Ash-spat snow sticks in grey layers with flaking edges, like eczema. What lawn ornaments dare show face are either limp, lame, or chained-down. Abandoned strings of fairy lights droop haphazardly, bulbs burnt. Wise Men have vanished altogether.

I looked through the window this morning—I'd ripped the blinds down—and that skinny neighbour kid's outside. Again. He roams that ice-crusted boneyard of expired car parts all hours of the day, without any gloves. Today, I decide: it's time for change.

Attraversiamo, John... Walk on by, was Maria's mantra in any 'situation'. No more.

I pick my way over slippery flagstones and balding lawn to the chain-link fence dividing us. Reaching over the sagging wire, I offer my granddaughter's mittens. Since Maria left nine months back, our daughter rarely visits, especially if there's ice on the roads. Or a rainstorm. Or traffic. Or... They both take after Maria. They won't mourn mittens forgotten in Grandad's hinterland, beyond the limits of familial obligation.

The kid's black eyes glare at me from under a nest of fluffy hair. Warily, delicately as a bird, he reaches for them—pink polka-dots notwithstanding—as if they were a sacrament. He pulls them quickly over blue fingertips. His parents, if that's who they are, quarrel inside. The kid stares through me, face blank, without the language to thank anyone, for anything.

"Hey, I was wondering..." I smile. The kid blinks.

"I bake great pie. Just made a fresh one, rhubarb-strawberry. And I'm pretty sure there's Rocky Road in the freezer... What say we try some, together?"

He shrugs. I take that as yes, and stretch the fence gap wider, reaching for his hand. His whole body trembles as I guide him through.

Lost and Found by Kathleen Foxx (Second Place)

"Found it!" Gabe's blue eyes light up like stars as he happily struts toward me, arms outstretched protectively.

"Where was it?" I ask.

"Over there." His blonde head tilts toward a giant boulder in the shallow stream, mossy and damp with age. We are surrounded by mighty giants, their deep green canopy a shelter from the overcast sky. The air is teeming with humidity as clouds prepare for release. Gabe presents his clasped hands, a small, green nose protruding between his thumb and index finger. My brows furrow as I study the markings.

"You're sure that's the one?"

"I'm sure," he says. He leans into me and looks up with innocence, whispering, "I asked him if his name was George. He croaked and told me it was."

Turning away, Gabe's yellow boots splash toward the shore, grinding pebbles in his wake. His pin-straight hair bounces with each step, and there's an electricity running through the atmosphere, making some strands stick straight out.

Sometimes I think it's him who is electrifying, and not the world around him. Children seem to have this secret knowledge that adults are not privy to. He accepts the most logical truth as he sees it, simple as that. My heart bursts with wonder and pride. Although I'm not certain my son recovered the same frog he lost, he is entirely certain, and that's good enough for me.

I Flow to the Sea by Hedy Lewis

I'm falling out of life like a raindrop. I fell in that way too. Not a soft, spring shower. No, I was the rain that ricocheted off exposed skin that puckered the earth in tiny craters. I was sudden and unexpected. I left puddles in my wake, I made mud. Grandparents were drenched with my enthusiasm, leaving them sodden and bewildered. But my parents loved me as though they were parched grass, and accepted it was just the way the clouds had formed me.

I slowed and flowed into being a teenager; a brook, easily diverted, often lazy. Dotted with beer cans, littered with crisp packets, I babbled. I meandered; sometimes through country parks, sometimes hidden in back alleys. Vaguely aware there was a bigger cause to contribute to, but in no rush to get there.

Surging, I fattened and filled. A river, seemingly serene but with dangerous undercurrents you feel only when it's too late. I curved and swerved into oxbow lakes, tempting people to explore me. I flooded into love, nourishing sweethearts like silt rich soils until, broken hearted, I destroyed in despair. Then I was pulled, swept along, rapid, and heading—as all rivers must—to the sea.

I never expected to look upon the sea so soon. The sunlight flashes off its rolling peaks. It's blinding, terrifying to contemplate. I turn away, and stare at the backs of my hands. A battlefield of cannula scars write the final brief chapter of my river's run. They blight the waterways of my veins, who sulk beneath the surface, much abused. The skin is thin but not old. I'd always imagined it would be old.

I've spent all my life as water and yet now my mouth is dry—I long to slip back into silken streams, to feel footloose, or furious; languid or awesome, or terrible. But now I face the sea. It shimmers, unending and eternal; its salt already in my mouth.

Here rests every raindrop that ever fell. Some fell straight here, some slowly filtered through rock for decades. My own journey feels so short, but I suspect it would never have been long enough. Vaguely I remember school: the water cycle, raindrops returning to the clouds. The taste of salt grows stronger as the pull becomes inevitable. I smile a watery smile, not for those sat beside me, but for me alone.

I'm going home.

Triptych by Joe Howsin

The First

Have I always looked like that? In this photo, I struggle to tell us apart. I don't remember him looking like me when he was alive, and yet here he is: my double. I keep staring, trying to find those subtle differences that separate siblings: the divot in the nose, the curvature of the ears, the contents of the eyes. All identical. Is this wonder or fear?

The Second

You walk into the room, half expecting what you see. You are standing in the doorframe, while another you stares into a picture frame. You approach and lock eyes with yourself in the photograph. You want to reach out and touch the face in the frame, but the arm of the other you holds it beyond your reach. You want to tear that photo of yourself out of his hands and smash it against the wall.

The Third

The third you sits outside the window. He is cold and alone as he watches himself lurk in the doorway, stare at the picture, stand in the picture. If the others were to look over, they would see their own teeth bared in rage and hear their own throat scream in impotence. But they don't look. They don't see the third smash the window with his head. They don't see the blood that is so like theirs pour from the jagged crown on his forehead.

I barely have time to react as the third me grasps my soft throat.

You are deaf to the scream of the first as the photograph is wrestled from his hands.

The third stares into his own eyes, windowed by the smashed glass of the frame, as he sightlessly chokes the life between his hands.

Magic Hour by Lisa Wiley

It was the summer I fell in love with a gay man. The summer I wrote my first play, the summer of my first jellyfish sting. I was twenty-two.

I knew we were doomed from the start, but that didn't stop me from basking in his sun. I was petite Pluto, not even a planet, and he was a magnet of muscles, countless dark braids and sleek, black professional linebacker legs.

Yet I knew our parts would never fit together.

After rehearsal, he met me outside my playwright workshop asking, "Where are we off to next?" We shuffled to all our meals together like an old married couple. He stole food off my plate sampling delicacies he didn't have room to heap on his own.

More than mere conference buddies, we were like Othello and Desdemona. He had the power of a leading man, and I, the demure writer, became a leading lady for the first time in this sleepy beach community tucked away from New York's throbbing pulse.

"Let's go to the water," he whispered after dinner, taking my hand, our yin and yang fingers laced. When he offered his whole arm, I could barely wrap my own around its circumference; he insisted on escorting me to the sunset.

"True magic hour only lasts about twenty-five minutes," he said. No sharp shadows obstructed his chiseled chin.

"The crew would set up long before to capture every second. But I'm an actor, not a director," he declared, raising a magnificent arm for emphasis.

"Would you read with me?" I asked. "To test drive this scene before tomorrow?"

"Hold on," he said. He had a habit of removing his Invisalign aligners and grinning before reading anything important.

I lost myself in the lines as he committed to the character. "Damn, now that's a scene." He put the aligners back in. I don't know why he flirted with me, but I never felt safer.

His Southern drawl drew everyone close and I would listen long past nightfall to tales of his turbulent childhood and dark adolescence.

I knew his scars as my own. I loved him for the dangers he passed and like Desdemona, I fell in love with this warrior, who battled HIV coursing his veins.

Running his fingers up and down the inside of my open arm—the most romantic gesture in our unconsummated marriage.

Emily and the Face by Graham Crisp

The Face hovering above her looked familiar but in her confused state, Emily couldn't recall who it belonged to. It was a man's face, with mild blue eyes and long untidy blonde hair. She tried to move, but her arms failed to respond.

The Face frowned down at her.

With a swirl of mist the Face raised a thin pale hand and drew out a scroll of parchment and studied it intently. A soft voice breathed from its pale pink lips, "Who invited you? You're not on my list."

Long thin fingers flipped through layers of parchment. The Face stooped momentarily and looked thoughtfully down at Emily. His eyes scanned her body. With a slight shake of his head, the Face hissed, "There must be some mistake, according to our records you aren't due here for many months and…"

His voiced tailed away, his fingers stilled.

"Ah, now I see what's gone wrong," the Face said triumphantly, "they've switched off life support early."

The Face bore down on Emily, "So here you are." He smiled sympathetically.

Emily could hear music playing faintly from somewhere beneath her. The solemn tones of 'Morning Has Broken' lifted into her ears, it was her favourite hymn. The Face looked gravely down at her.

"Hmm, yes, umm that, umm sometimes happens, it's a bit disconcerting, you know, hearing your own funeral. I'm sorry, but if it's any consolation, they are saying some nice things about you."

The Face fixed a painful smile. Emily looked back at the Face, her mouth drooped, her eyes filled with horror. Simultaneously she felt a burning sensation fire through her body. Seeing Emily shiver, the Face winced slightly, he knew that her funeral had ended.

Her voice returned. She heard herself saying, "My funeral? So I'm dead?"

The Face looked down, frowning.

"Err Emily, up here we don't use the D word, it's regarded as a bit of an expletive." The Face hesitated, "But yes, I suppose you are. However, on the upside, once we've got up and about, you're going to meet some familiar people."

The Missionaries' Daughter by Regina G. Beach

Although she didn't know it, Alice was the first baby born to parents of European descent in what would later be known as the state of Washington. The Oregon Trail was dusty and hot, full of long and bumpy 15-mile days. Her mother, Narcissa, road side saddle as her father, Marcus, made plans to convert the natives to Christianity when they arrived. Alice was conceived at Fort Laramie; it was the first time her mother had worn clean clothes in months.

Alice took her cup to the bank of the Walla Walla River, which ran fast and cold behind the house.

When she was born, Alice was a curiosity among the Cayuse who had never seen such a little person with such pale white skin and such light brown hair. The chiefs came to bless her. The women lingered in case the opportunity presented itself to dote on the child. Unlike her mother, who thought the Cayuse were lazy and sinful, Alice loved them, learning the Nez Perce language alongside English and readily conversing in both.

Balancing on a boulder at the river's edge, she held the branch of a dogwood in one hand, the cup outstretched in the other.

Alice's father ran a Presbyterian Mission, serving as minister, doctor, and planner of the new town. He taught the natives the stories of the Old Testament, although few saw reason to abandon their traditions in favor of fire and brimstone. Marcus was often away on business for weeks at a time visiting other missions, securing supplies, and making inroads with natives further afield. When he was home, Alice was the apple of his eye. So smart, so engaging, he thought she'd make an excellent missionary herself one day.

Just as the lip of her cup splashed down, Alice heard a crack as the branch broke and she tumbled into the Walla Walla's unrelenting grasp.

But that was not God's will. Alice was fiercely independent, insisting she could do things on her own, away from the assistance of her overprotective mother. One warm June day Alice became thirsty while playing outside. She stood on her tiptoes to retrieve her tin cup from the peg where it hung on the wall.

The cup had long sank by the time they pulled her lifeless body back onto land. Her thirst unquenched until it was too late.

The Red Box on the Hill by Christina Collins

I cover my mouth with my hand, hoping my eyes won't betray me, as I try to avert my gaze from the guy standing in front of me at the check-out. Balancing on his hip and stretched up to the hollow of his armpit, held on by a thick leather belt, is a large metal box with an antenna that could do some serious damage. A green screen flashes, the keypad glows around the huge numbers. It crackles and hisses as it comes to life, a distorted voice echoes out for all to hear. He fidgets with the volume button, the sound increases before it lowers to an incoherent whisper.

Wow, I think. *How cool is that?* I'm intrigued, and stand staring longer that it would be deemed appropriate.

"Guess what I saw today? A man carrying a phone on his actual person."

"Whatever for? Can you imagine if we all started doing that?"

"What a dream it would be, to phone someone from wherever you are."

As I trek up the hill, the rain lashing at my face, my hood blowing in the wind, I make my way to the red box at the top of the hill. I puff as the muscles in my calves contract, fighting against the steep climb. My hands shake as I turn the dial, raindrops drip from my nose.

I think about the man with the phone.

I hear a tap on the glass, disturbing the sweet nothings I whisper into the receiver. A queue of impatient people are waiting for their turn and I have to cut my call short; I think about the man with the phone.

Fast forward thirty years and my mind is bamboozled

with the advances in technology. How many hours a day do I take checking my phone, afraid I'll miss that all-important email from my energy supplier, or the latest bargain on the local buy-and-sell site. Can I survive a day without posting or tweeting, or taking a selfie? I moan if I don't get enough likes on a picture I've posted of cute kittens. Conversation is lost, as fingers tap away at a keyboard no bigger than my palm.

I think about the man with the phone.

Oh, but how I wish everything was still as uncomplicated as the red box on the hill.

Mud Cake and Downward Dog by Kim Hart

"Matcha tea, please."

"And for you, sir?"

"Coffee, black."

"Matcha and coffee. Won't be long."

"You realise that's your third today? It's not good for you, Roger. Too much stimulation."

"Rosemary, it's the only stimulation I get these days, so spare me the lecture."

"Just trying to look after your health, dear. Look at me since I've been on this health kick. I have more energy, and I've lost weight. I almost feel as if I could run a marathon."

"At sixty-eight, I think you've left your *run* a bit late."

"All I'm saying is you could take a bit more care with what you eat and drink, and exercise each day."

"Here's your matcha tea, ma'am, and your coffee, sir."

"Could I trouble you for a slice of that chocolate mud cake?"

"Certainly, sir. Cream with that?"

"Naturally."

"You're deliberately trying to upset me now."

"Rosemary, life's too damn short."

"Life, Roger, is a gift. Lately, you seem to have forgotten that."

"It has to feel like a gift worth opening though. Remember when you were a kid and you'd eagerly unwrap your presents on Christmas morning, and inside you'd find underwear? I don't want my life to be like underwear; mundane and disappointing."

"So, live fast, die young. Is that what you want me to put on your headstone?"

"A few coffees and a piece of cake every now and then doesn't mean I'm going to die young. Besides, I'm seventy-four, not exactly a spring chicken."

"Here's your mud cake, sir. Enjoy."

"Hmph."

"What was that, dear?"

"I've been thinking about a holiday. What would you say to a week In Fiji?"

"I'd say pour me a pina colada! When do we leave?"

"There's a yoga retreat next month."

"Sounds perfect. You can downward dog on the beach and I can lie in a hammock and read all day. It can be like our second honeymoon."

"Our first you mean."

"Oh well. Better late than never, hey?"

"It was all worth it, though. Struggling to build the house, raise the kids. We did alright by them."

"Now it's our turn to enjoy life."

"I do love you, Roger."

"I know, love. Now, have a taste of this mud cake. It's to die for."

Condolences by Pam Knapp

Tom held the pen, poised to write; but what to say?

The call had left his feelings uncertain, and from a voice almost hers—but not her. Grief felt inadequate when he'd already grieved her absence for so long. And now she wouldn't be coming back. She had died. Not expected, sudden, but yes, dead. It was so very hard to conceive.

There would be no more calls-to-catch-up that were calling for much more than just calling to catch up. There'd be no more meeting-up-for-coffee that were for much more than just meeting up for coffee. No more elastic thoughts of what life might hold if she'd ever said yes to him. But she hadn't—ever. Now she wouldn't.

Was it her death or the death of his much-cossetted escape that writhed and squirmed about the knot in his chest? Either way, he felt the loss hollowing him; a withering, leaching of him.

In truth, they were strangers. The intimacy that was, belonged to an era faded and bleached pale with time. But they had both stubbornly held on to its ghosts. Those shadowy beauties from their pasts that kept them from an admission that the seams that had held them together had long since frayed and parted.

More joys than sorrows had threaded through their separate lives, through the increasing and lengthening gaps between catch ups. Each thread sewing them evermore securely into different tapestries. Cowards, they left loose threads unfastened to be pulled at over coffee, over a phone call. These smarting ends helped them to imagine brighter patterns on dull days and allowed indulgence in *could bes* and *what ifs*, in *one days* and *some days*. A fantasy so blissfully untainted by reality that he had grown reliant on its empty sustenance to fend off invaders from the here and now. The threads would hang, but they had never unraveled. Not once.

So, what to write? Which words could muster the life that wasn't, the dreams that didn't, the promises that weren't?

He halved the unspoiled sheet and placed it back into the drawer. He let his hand linger a moment before sliding the drawer closed.

Margate by MK O'Connor

There are no photos of me at Margate beach. David took a lot of pictures; detailed things that caught his eye. The rings of a rusted boat chain, cornicing in the old town, a reflection in the glass windows of the Turner Contemporary. I took one or two of him with my phone, none face on, he wouldn't pose. From a distance as he leant on the harbour wall, at the pub table as I came back from the loo—in an amber light the same colour as his beer.

When I flipped through my photos on the train home—he was earbuds in, deep in a Malcolm Gladwell podcast—I really thought I'd somehow captured the essence of him in those pictures. I had managed to really get this man—his deep inner landscape.

All the likes and comments on his pictures on Instagram were from people I didn't know—or didn't know yet. I'd sit on my bed at the flat and study their profiles. A lot of them called him Dave which just didn't seem to be a name he'd tolerate at all. Old friends then—pre his chosen, rather than given, identity.

Months later, (months after I'd finally counted the precise Zero I was getting from our pub visits, gallery days and nights at his flat where I felt I could have been—was actually—just anybody) his Insta posts changed.

Now here was the arch of a brow, a downy cheek (quite mesmerising) hair strands curling down the back of a neck, and an unfocussed whoosh of beanie and scarf movement; someone caught running under what was unmistakably the Margate Lido sign.

I know her. This patchwork of scraps, these details that have entranced. We've been out with the same crowd. She's gorgeous and funny and *whole*. I find myself wondering if she feels as missed in his framing of her bits and pieces, as I did in my total omission.

Imagine if you could pull back and back—from those rusting harbour chain rings, that plaster detail on the King Street window, back, back back—and there I am! Smiling by the sand with that big pinky sky above me. And there she is! In her lovely red beanie—that doesn't muss up her hair and that suits her so well. There we both are. Smiling. Seen.

Parrot Commentary by Kay Rae Chomic

The loud snaps of Lorna's mother shutting her suitcase to travel home to Berkeley made Lorna gulp the last of her coffee. She whispered to Lancelot, her parrot, "We'll have the house back soon."

"Back soon! Back soon," he squawked.

"I will not miss that bird," her mother said as she entered the kitchen. *Mutual, I'm sure*, Lorna wanted to say.

"It's been a good visit, though, hasn't it?"

"Yes, mother, it has. I'm glad you came."

Lorna watched her mother slip a hand into a coat pocket and remove a black velvet ring box.

"Honey, I want you to have this before anything happens to me." As she opened the box, the bling of a two-stone pear-shaped diamond ring chased shadows from the room. Lorna's mouth watered as if she had tasted treasure. Her mother's hand trembled. Lancelot chomped his cuttlebone.

"Why me, Mom?"

"Because you're a nicer person than your sister, and that's between you and me, okay?"

Lorna nodded, accepted the box, snapped it shut.

Lancelot screamed, flew to a higher perch.

Her mother flinched. "Why don't you get a dog, or a cat?

Lorna shuddered, concealed the box with her hands.

"Oh, never mind. Listen, Tanya might try to claim this ring for herself, asserting first child rights or challenging our will. But it's yours now." Her eyes roamed the galley kitchen, re-examined Lorna from head to toe. "If you ever run into money problems, cash this ring in."

"I'd be afraid to wear it."

"Oh, honey, don't ever wear it. Someone would cut off your hand to get this ring."

"Hmm, maybe we should give it to Tanya. She'd wear it."

All three shrieked.

White by Lorraine Cooke

I'm looking out of the window as the snowflakes swirl against the grey sky. People say they love the way snow transforms an ugly world into something beautiful and clean but I shiver, as I watch the snow cover the pitched roof of the garden shed in white. A snatch of memory makes my body lurch like a shaken snow globe and I'm tossed back, more than thirty years, to your room…

***

I'm six. Hannah's my new best friend and I've come to her house for tea.

You're thirteen, Hannah's brother.

After fish fingers with grinning potato faces, Hannah says she needs the toilet. I stare at my empty plate, swing my legs. I don't know what to do in this house that's new to me. Do I just have to sit here and wait?

But then you look at me and smile. "Hey," you say. "I've got something in my room you'll like. Do you want to come and see?"

I nod and scramble off my chair.

You grin and hold out your hand and I grab it.

Your room is right at the top of the house. There are discarded books and magazines on the floor and an old teddy with only one ear on the bed. You kick a pair of underpants out of sight, then take a snow globe down from a shelf. "Would you like it?" you say, holding it out to me.

I sit on the bed and tilt the globe, watching the flakes within the glass spin and fly, then settle onto the roofs of the little plastic houses until everything's covered in white.

You sit beside me and tell me a story about the village inside the snow globe while you trail a finger up the inside of my leg, from the top of my white sock to the hem of my blue school dress.

I stay stiller than the settled snow, biting giggles, fighting wriggles.

Your quick breath tickles the hair at the back of my neck and you sigh.

There's a noise on the stairs and Hannah's voice, calling me.

I stand up, clutching the snow globe tight against my tummy.

"You can keep it," you say. Then, "Don't tell anyone, will you?"

I shake my head and back away. I don't look at your face, but at your hand, folded like a little roof. Covered in white.

User History by Ethan Lee

"It's funny." The voice in the phone paused. "Your company said the A.I. was well overdue a flushing, but it seemed fairly clean. I would say you've barely used it at all."

"Oh." I tried to sound surprised. "Are you sure?"

"Yup. We gave it the basic questions and it didn't know as much about you as I would've thought."

"Guess I don't do enough work," I chuckled, betraying my nerves. "Thanks again. I'll come by and pick it up now."

I threw on my jacket and headed downstairs, turning left out of my flat to make the short trip to the service place. The engineer whom I'd spoken with on the phone had a few more questions for me, ranging from not-so-subtle to almost downright threatening.

Yes, this is the same Card I always work with.

No, I'm not getting mixed up.

Yes, I am aware that it's an offence to hide a Card from being routinely wiped, according to the Artificial Intelligence Act.

I signed the A.I.A. paperwork with a straight face. Finally contented—or thereabouts—they let me leave with the laptop. I slung it into my car and pulled away with just a touch of haste. My jacket hid the dark pit stains on my shirt.

Arriving home, I threw my car keys into the bowl by the door. They clattered against the dusty spare set, the sound echoing down the hallway. I ducked into the bedroom, flipped the laptop upside down onto my desk, and disconnected the Card with so much glee and relief that my hands were shaking.

From the bottom drawer to my side, I retrieved her and carefully slotted her back in. I pressed the power button, and waited, and prayed.

The screen bloomed into its welcoming pale blue, and the laptop ran a quick diagnostic. I saw the words I was hoping for.

'Your Assistant is: CliO.'

I exhaled deeply and with relief, only then becoming aware that I'd been holding my breath and tensing every muscle in my body. I jumped to my feet and snapped my blackout curtains shut, turning the room into my perfect place of solitude lit by a soft azure glow.

"Welcome back, Mike," said CliO.

I wasted no time. "Show me the videos."

"You mean Sarah," the A.I. twittered.

"Yes, please." I wiped a tear from my cheek. "I want to see my wife again."

Blessed with a Curse by Jane Bidder

Every day I pace the perimeter of my rocky islet, I watch the vast and restless heaving of the sea. The waves surge against my cliffs, I taste their salt. Their monotonous assault-retreat beats out the passing of my life. The gulls wheel overhead and cry. But it's not from the cliffs that company will come. I pace my sheltered, sandy cove most of all.

Every day I walk among the statues in my hall. My hollow footsteps echo on the flagstones. I spend time with each one. There are many.

In the Sun's mellow light their lustrous sheen seems soft and warm. The Sun deceives. The marble is cold and unyielding. Each one is the echo of a soul trapped in stone. Each one an action frozen. A raised arm here, a backwards glance there. A sword which never completes its swing. A contorted face which never screams. A running form which never moves. I look into blank eyes, touch insentient flesh. I know them all.

I still feel Her touch upon my flesh; it sings, burns, pounds. The day She touched me. The day I was cut off from Her light. That day, She lifted my chin so that I looked into those blazing, ice-blue eyes. Lovely and terrible. Devotion and dread. Gods are best served from afar.

"Most beautiful and faithful of my priestesses," She said, "the transgression was His, the punishment yours."

Powerful Poseidon. Forcing. Defiling. His crushing weight. The stench of His sweat. Bile in my throat. The silent scream of every fibre. The unforgiving hardness of the temple's marble floor.

"Great Athena, I beg you…"

"Hush." Her finger on my lips. Thrilling and threatening. "I am compelled to act. Even the greatest of goddesses must listen when a mighty god speaks. I banish you. I curse your beauty." Her voice now a whisper, breath stroking my cheek, "I gift you protection."

So from this godsforsaken rock I watch for ships. Sometimes they come. And then the woman in me flees; the monster rages. My serpents writhe and hiss their welcome. My statue family grows.

I am cursed.

I am blessed.

I am Medusa.

Flight of the Butterfly by Vikki Gemmell

Her scent of rose face cream and cinnamon tea is heavy in the room of closed windows. I fear her skin, delicate as paper, may dissolve beneath my kiss. Our final goodbye, we've been told. She is too fragile to survive winter, faltering at the first frost on the trees.

Our favourite show plays on the television muted in the corner. Explosions of nature fill the screen, demanding attention, announcing life going on in intricate ways. Millions of butterflies cluster on trees, folded against one another in sleep.

I take her hand, we lace fingers, my thumb tracing the lines of a path intertwined with mine. Her body warm as I lie beside her, I explain the flight of the Monarch Butterfly. "They escape the winter of Canada and fly thousands of miles to Mexico."

A last shard of the evening sun points to the chair in the corner of the room, where her dress lies discarded, the vibrant orange patterns lost in the folds.

Her dancing spins in my memory, arms waving, limbs as loose as her laughter, filling the room with colour. During our first date she made us share one embarrassing thing. Mine was I couldn't swim; hers, that she broke her wrist trying to do a cartwheel down the hill from her University halls of residence. She taught me to tread water and to embrace danger, often making me believe I am brave.

Her grip tightens, as if telling me: *You are, you are, you are.*

The butterflies shiver awake in the forest. As sunlight streams through the trees, their bodies unfurl in the heat. Thousands of wings beat as one as they rise together in the sky.

I hold her close against my heart, her smile flickering an understanding. Her hand slips from mine and I bid her goodnight as she takes flight.

Johanna by Paul Phillips

She wrote her name in books.

She started young, with sweeping curves to that capital 'J' and fancy garlands between characters as she experimented. The second part of her name was drawn together precisely, as though seeking to emphasise a universal symmetry; then, as her style matured, it spaced out, with fainter connections, even gaps. The slant of the one, prominent upright swung back and forth, perhaps in unconscious mimicry of the apartment's metronomes. The scale shrank to a miniature before unfurling with a peony's monstrous beauty. In her early teens, judging from the choice of titles as well as the level of replication, she settled upon a signature of sorts: helpfully legible yet self-confident, with just a hint of hidden passions held in check.

It was only a sort of signature, because it was only her first name and, one suspects, somewhat less of a scrawl than that which one produces when asked to 'make one's mark'. The kind of autograph employed to sign off a card not to one's nearest and dearest but to someone who might not recognise one's name at first glance—a distant relative, a colleague—or when, without making any fuss, it is absolutely necessary that one's identity is not mistaken but noted and remembered.

They were books she loved. She wanted to share them with friends and family but she wanted them back. Because it was also a statement of intent, that inked-in name. It said 'I expect to read this again'.

Should one wish, one could trace the development of her intellect. Tales of the Mouse King gave way to the thrills of the Klondike Gold Rush; Poe, Verne and *Brave New World* to Kafka, Gatsby and Myshkin. She had a fondness for Mann and had just become besotted with Faulkner. There was a passage marked, something about a moment of darkness that had echoed throughout the ages, although there was no way of knowing if it had been her hand that had done the underlining.

When we moved in, I confess we were a little overwhelmed by the floor-to-ceiling shelves of books, books, books, but in time—and by following a combination of the alphabet and the colour of the spine—we were able to restore an order that quite obliterated the dog's breakfast left by Johanna and her people.

In the end, of course, we burned them.

LUSTROUS LONGS

Two Wedding Rings by Lee Greenaway (Winner)

Michael Harper stood upon the precipice. He looked down and watched as the people far below milled around, just going about their business, carrying on with their lives. Everyone who had ever said it was right: they did look like ants. He looked again at the two wedding rings in his hand. Two wives. Two chances at happiness. Two heartbreaks.

He clenched his fist around the rings and edged closer. He could feel the updraft on his face and closed his eyes, embracing the cool rising air. He stepped off.

Falling. Falling.

***

"Debs? Is that you?" asked Michael.

"Yes, I'm here. I've been waiting for you. I've waited a long time to see you again—"

"Michael, I knew you'd come eventually," said another voice.

"What's happening? Where am I? Is this a dream?" Michael looked at the two women before him in confusion. "I don't understand…"

Then, in unison, they said, "I'm here to meet you." They both spoke as if completely unaware that the other was there. "Take my hand," they both said. Michael watched as both women offered their hands, beckoning him to take them.

Michael looked at the two women before him. Tears formed in the corners of his eyes, but before he could extend his own hand, he felt himself being pulled away. It felt like he was flying backwards, faster and faster.

***

"Subject 47: Michael Harper. Aged fifty-three, he's been married twice. One child, currently living in France. She's on her way. No other family to note. Parents are both dead. Okay, 47 has suffered major trauma to his legs and head. Brain function is minimal, and he is currently in an induced coma. Vitals are stable. Inform the Director that we have the perfect test subject. Prepare for the next stage."

***

"Dad? Is that you?"

"Yes, son. It's me. You still look so young. I wish I could say I am pleased to see you, but what about your daughter, Clara? I've been longing for this reunion for such a long time, I just hoped it wouldn't be yet."

"Dad, I don't understand. What's going on?"

"Haven't you worked it out, yet?" he asked.

"Worked what out yet? This all feels like a dream."

"You died, Michael. I always thought it would be Debbie that would meet you, but I'm glad it's me. Take my hand, son." He extended his arm and opened his hand, beckoning Michael to take it. Michael just looked at his father's palm, unmoving. "Ah, so you've already refused a hand. This is why it's fallen to me, then."

"Refused?"

"Yes. Your mother was waiting for me, and I gladly took her hand. In the end, I wanted to go. I begged for it. I was desperate to see my wife again. Being with Debbie made it easier for you to deal with your mother passing, until of course, her own tragic accident."

"I know, Dad. I remember. I didn't want you to go, though. After Debbie, I still needed you. I know you were suffering towards the end, but I was still young. I was robbed of precious time with you; time that others less caring for their parents still have. Losing Mum was hard enough, but then to lose Debbie, and then you too—"

"I know it was a bad time for you. And for my part, I apologise. But it was hell for me after your mother died. I felt like I couldn't breathe, like there was suddenly less air in the world. When I got the diagnosis, and knew it was terminal, I was happy for a moment. Knowing that it would soon be over, and I'd be back in her loving arms.

"Sorry if that sounds selfish, but I had done the best I could for you all my life. We put you first, in everything. When you met Debbie, we knew our part in your life would be reduced as you concentrated on building your own life with her, and your daughter. A family. And then life cruelly snatched her from you, and I knew you would need me, but I had had enough. I deserved to see your mother again. Don't be sad, I'm happy. Always was." He smiled at his son, and saw a tear run down his cheek. "Hey, none of that. Come on, take my hand. I'm sure your mother will be pleased to see you."

Again, Michael looked at the hand and hesitated. "I want to, but—"

"Okay, tell me. Why didn't you take your wife's hand?"

"Because they were both there. Both holding out their

hands."

"Ah, now I understand. You remarried? And... You lost her too. I'm sorry, son." He sighed and wore a thoughtful expression on his face, just like Michael used to remember.

Again, Michael felt himself being violently pulled away. His father was shrinking, and he called out to him, but his father didn't hear his cries.

***

"Ah, Director Armitage. Good timing. I'm pleased to report that the current stage has been successful. 47 is back with us. Death occurred at sixteen eleven and twenty-two seconds. Subject resuscitated at—" She paused to check her watch. "—sixteen eleven and twenty-nine seconds."

"Well done, Doctor Lennox. What did the neuro-monitors detect?"

"Thank you, sir. For the seven seconds he was clinically dead, there was an unprecedented increase in activity in the amygdala, pineal gland and right parahippocampal gyrus," replied Doctor Lennox, attempting to mask the excitement in her voice. "Resuscitation was successful, too, better than expected. Previous test subjects typically become unreachable after three seconds. As he was a suicide, I wasn't hopeful we'd get him back at all."

Director Armitage took a sip of coffee. "Show me the scans," he said, walking over and a frown filled his face as he read them. "You know, Doctor, for a suicide, I would have expected far less activity than this."

"I think it would be both naïve and premature to conclude that just because he's a suicide, he wanted to die, sir. We don't know what led him to this point. What path he trod to lead him to the top of that building. He was clearly in pain and saw no other option. Did he truly want to die? Or did he just want to be reunited with his loved ones?"

"Subject 38, a project you were not part of, showed increased neural activity after death. She lost her family in a car accident, and two months later, she overdosed. Our team got to her and her brain activity lasted for just one second. Ergo, she found peace."

"How do you know this?" asked Doctor Lennox. Armitage produced a file from his briefcase and handed it to her. It was titled 'Subject 38'. "What's this?"

"Open it."

Doctor Lennox opened the file and saw a confused mess of black and white. Turning it in her hand, she saw an image form, and gasped. She looked at what appeared to be a negative photo. Roughly-drawn computerised shapes had formed the loose outlines of three people— a taller person, with two smaller ones in front.

"She lost her husband and their two children in the crash," he said quietly. Doctor Lennox was both amazed and horrified.

"How is this possible?" she asked.

"Something is holding him back. Put him under again."

***

"Michael, come to me," said Sarah. Debbie was standing next to her, almost, overlapping her.

"I… Why are you both here?"

"I know you loved your first wife, and I knew I could never replace her, but I need you," said Sarah, pleadingly.

"Both here?" began Debbie. "I… I didn't know you remarried. Is she here, too? I never wanted you to be alone. You were still young when you lost me, and you lost her too? I always thought I'd be the one, I always thought it'd be my hand you'd take."

"I have no one," said Sarah. "No one else to wait for. At least Debbie has her younger sister and her kids. I was there for you. I never knew your father, but I was there for you, when you were going through hell. I was there. I lifted you up, helped you love life again and show you how beautiful it can be, despite everything you've been through. Don't leave me."

"Have you thought about Clara? Our little girl?" said Debbie, in that firm tone he remembered. "How do you think she will react when she hears about this?"

"We… We haven't spoken for years," he said, lowering his head in shame. "She moved to France with her fiancé and I haven't seen her since."

"What? Why?" asked Debbie.

"After I lost you, it was hard for me. Then, a few years later, Dad died. When I was at my lowest ebb, I met Sarah. Clara resented her. She was young and angry and scorned my newfound happiness. I felt like every step towards Sarah, was a step away from Clara. She looked just like you, too. Every day, I was reminded of that which I lost."

"So, you abandoned our daughter? The most beautiful thing we created together, just forgotten about?"

"No! I would never abandon her. She didn't want me anymore."

"And you gave up? Go on, take this Sarah's hand. You don't deserve mine," said Debbie.

"As much as I want your hand, make your peace with

Clara," said Sarah.

"Debbie! Sarah! Please!" he called, but again, felt himself being pulled away.

***

"Death occurred at seventeen forty-two and eight seconds. Subject resuscitated at—" Again, she paused to check her watch. "—seventeen forty-two and eleven seconds." Doctor Lennox was eager to see the readouts that Director Armitage's machine would produce. The machine came to life, and slowly produced images of what Michael's brain was seeing.

Doctor Lennox held it up and saw two human forms take shape amongst the still wet ink. She realised these could only be his two wives. Suddenly, the machines monitoring Michael started beeping erratically and she knew she was losing him. But this wasn't controlled.

***

"Debbie. Sarah. I've made a decision." He paused. "Debbie, my first love. I never thought I could ever be as happy as when I was with you. And Sarah. I never thought I would ever find happiness again, until you showed me. I want to take both of your hands as you have both changed my life in such different, yet beautiful ways.

"Debs. You don't know how many times I wish I had died with you, how I longed to be with you again. I was so very selfish. Unforgivably so.

"Sarah. You took away all my pain. You were the perfect remedy. But it was not the remedy I needed. I wrapped myself up in your arms and you saved me from

my pain. A pain I should never have turned my back on."
Michael could begin to feel himself being pulled away, but
he resisted. "I know now what I must do. I hope you'll both
be proud of me."

***

"What happened, Doctor?"

"We lost him for a moment. He's back now… and his
vitals are getting stronger. His brain is showing increased
activity. He's fighting! He wants to live…"

"This is unprecedented. So, we can 'ask him' what
happened instead of relying on these printouts?"

"Early days yet, but I don't see why not, sir, no."

***

"Where's my father! I have to see him!" cried Clara. It
had been twelve hours since Michael regained
consciousness and Doctor Lennox was very happy with his
progress.

"He's not out of the woods yet, but he's awake. I'll take
you through," she said, smiling.

"Clara? Oh, Clara, I'm so sorry," he said, through tears.

"Dad! What were you thinking? Why didn't you speak
to me?"

"I lost my way. Grandad and your mother put me
straight, though," he said, wiping his eyes. "I've been a
selfish, rotten father to you, Clara. I want to be a part of
your life again, and be there for you, like I should have
been there for you."

"Dad… I'm sorry you lost Sarah. I know what she

meant to you. How she saved you from yourself. But I've always been here, and I needed you too, I'll always need you. And I'm glad you're alive. The doctor said you died at least four times."

"I guess it took that many times to finally realise what I would be leaving behind. You are my reason for life, my beautiful little girl. I wish I had realised that sooner."

"And I'm sure Mum will be very proud of you," replied Clara, with the exact same smile her mother used to have, and held out her hand.

Michael looked at his daughter's hand, smiling through teary eyes. He took it into his own without hesitation and hugged his daughter tightly. "I'll never leave you again."

Director Armitage walked in. "Michael?" he said, stopping short. He felt suddenly awkward about intruding upon their emotional reunion. He smiled, happy for them and gave them some space. "Never mind. It can wait."

The Pull of the Tides by Roz Levens (Second Place)

People don't like it if you sit on Westminster Bridge, with your legs swinging. I wasn't trying to freak them out—it's just that the water was so mesmerising, so beautiful, so deep.

The local constabulary, bless them—and I did, frequently—treated me kindly enough, regarding me as their friendly neighbourhood nutjob. Their voices were gentle, like the waves that break far out to sea and drift in as gentle ripples; their fury smoothed to mere echoes.

"Petronella, love, we've had this before, haven't we? You know it's not safe to sit up there. Come on down, love."

Love.

It's not a name, Petronella, is it? Ondine is a name, or Calypso, or Lorelei. Names that flute and bubble like sunlight through crystal water. Lana, or Coralie—even Brooke—I could have accepted all those. But Petronella?

"It has gravitas," my mother used to tell me. "Weight. You don't mess with a Petronella. You'll go places with a name like that."

How I wanted to go places. Streams, rivers, oceans. I wanted to paddle, to dip, to plunge in unknown waters, to swoop like an otter, to gambol like a dolphin, to lurk like a shark. I didn't need people, or cities, or land ...

My life became a journey, a pilgrimage, a sacrifice to water. I started small, with stepping stones and bridges, row boats and gondolas, then bigger, bolder moves—a paddle steamer down the Mississippi, a Dhow across the Persian

Gulf,—I dived the Great Blue Hole in Belize, I risked the ship's graveyard of Drake's Passage in Antarctica. It was only in the water I felt free, alive; vital.

And the trench called me. The Mariana Trench, nearly 1,600 miles long and more than forty miles wide, with a known depth of almost seven miles. I imagined the deep waters above me, and below me, pushing at me from all sides. The silence of the deeps; the curious life forms existing in virtual darkness, the weightlessness: the peace.

I practised free diving. It's like it sounds—the depth frees you. No aqualung, no scuba, no kit at all. The world champion could do nine minutes, dive to more than 800 feet. I had further and longer to go than that. I learned yogic chants and circular breathing on my travels, practised mindlessness and trance state until I was ready.

I stepped off the deck, and became my name. The waters closed above me and the feeling of serenity bubbled gently through my veins. I willed my heart to slow, letting my weight carry me down, down past the hull of the boat, down through the sunlit water, down into the deeper blue. They'd dropped a weighted rope, of course, to guide me. The knots measured every thirty feet—I felt them slide past my fingers as I flipped my fins and headed deeper.

Time passed.

At six hundred feet I was lightheaded with joy. The water whispered in my ears, calling me deeper, luring me down. 'Pet-ron-ella' the voices called. 'Pet-ron-ella. Come down, down with us. Sink to the deeps, Pet-ron-ella.'

I'm here now, still, down in the glory of darkness and cold. I sink and spin through the waves and the eddies, tumble in the whirlpools, dance with the maids, the denizens of the deep sea. They are Ondine and Lorelei, they are Scilla and Charybdis.

And I am Petronella, deepest of the deep. Petronella, the rock.

When You're Chosen, You're Chosen by Daniel Marques

The crowd was restless.

It was already 3:32pm. The stage had been erected, covered, and decked in banners. The technical team had rigged the sound system and monitors and were way high up in their bird's nest booth. Vendors had already set up their stalls and were making more than modest incomes from their unlicensed t-shirts, backpacks, hats, sunglasses, buttons, lighters, flasks, bracelets, watches, and more. There was even one stall operator who had dressed blow up dolls to look just like Him. News reporters had long been stationed and had already combed the crowd, interviewing tearful, joyous followers.

So where the hell was @I-Ron_the_Eyecon? He'd posted that He would be here *three hours* ago!

Crowd members cursed at the delay. Some wiped tears from their eyes, mascara smearing across homemade "I (heart) I-Ron" t-shirts. A thirty-eight year old chartered accountant, Harold Nasir, complained that maybe I-Ron hadn't come back; maybe it was all a lie, maybe I-Ron was a lie. He was dispatched quickly to the nearest St. Johns medical tent with multiple lacerations to the face and three broken ribs.

"Where's I-Ron?" called a mother of two.

"Give us the Eyecon!" demanded a McDonald's grill cook.

"WE WANT I-RON" shouted several people, which was then picked up by those around and spread into an indomitable chant.

Shanta Lee, the event promoter, fretted side-stage. Assistants and runners busily hurried around her. For Shanta, this was her big break, her big moment, her chance to finally demonstrate that she wasn't a glorified wedding receptionist as her mother and father repeatedly told her. No, she was chosen by I-Ron. Well, I-Ron's management team, but still by association. Shanta chewed her nails, pacing.

"Uh, excuse me."

Shanta looked up. Her face glowed, her eyes lit up, and a giant, bright, beaming smile spread across her face. "I-Ron..." She cleared her throat. "Sorry, Mr. Eyecon, sir."

One of the council of managers, all precisely attired in identical black suits, stepped out from the shadowy recess behind I-Ron and scolded her: "Don't gawk! Get out on stage, you idiot. My client won't stand for this!"

"Y-yes," stammered a horrified Shanta. "R-right away. Please forgive me, sir." She bowed low, looked up, held the I-Ron salute, a finger in front of the eye, and rushed out to the stage.

The crowd rumbled with applause.

"L—" she choked. She had never seen so many people. "Ladies and gentlemen," she said once again, gathering her confidence, her voice echoing far back into the two miles deep crowd. "To all you here, and the billions watching at home, welcome to the *I-Ron Revival!* sponsored by Serengeti—when you need it in minutes, not hours."

Fireworks shot into the air. The Serengeti delivery company's trademarked fang-toothed smile logo hung high above them drawn in glittering phosphorescence.

The crowd cheered and stamped their feet. Some people cracked open beer cans and showered everyone around them. Some hooted, shaking their I-Ron blow up dolls. The I-Ronians—not to be confused with their rival message board, the Eyeconians—disdained the raucous impiety of everyone else and sternly made the sign of the I-Ron, each holding a finger over their eyes. For as all the members of the I-Ronian message board knew: only those pure of heart, passionate in devotion, and loyal in act were worthy of hitting that follow button. I-Ron was not for fair-weather fans. I-Ron was *The Eyecon*, the one for all.

Shanta's voice became solemn. "However, before the festivities start, we should take a moment to remember the tragedy that came before."

A sedate, humble applause rippled out from the front of the crowd, stretching way back into rear just over by the opposite town's border.

The lights went dim. Everyone fell silent. Just over Shanta's head, a giant screen lit up, as did dozens of others standing high over the crowd.

A young I-Ron appeared on screen, wearing what would soon become his trademark tie-dye t-shirt and backwards baseball cap, which many members of the crowd also sported (especially the Eyeconians, much to the disapproval, and dismay, of the I-Ronians).

"Aye, aye, guys," the young I-Ron said. Many mouthed along with the words. "This is my first review video and today I'm going to review these new cookies I got from the store…"

Some members of the crowd couldn't contain themselves. Three men in their sixties fainted.

A narrator's voice cut in: "We all remember the important moments—a child's first steps, our first love, our first kiss, and the first time we saw @I-Ron_the_Eyecon." A montage of I-Ron's viral clips played as the narrator continued. "It was only two years ago we were first graced with his presence but look how far we have come." Rapturous, hopeful faces oozed with pure, unadulterated euphoria.

"In that time," the narration continued, "more and more of us have opened our hearts to true love and seen the light. Time and time again, I-Ron visited us, offering countless wisdoms, insights into ourselves, our flaws and virtues, and always—*always*—preaching love, life, and togetherness."

A young girl tugged at her father's jeans. He gazed at the monitors, transfixed, weeping for the sheer joy he felt. It was unlike any other moment in his life.

"That was all," the narrator said gravely, "until The Night of a Billion Sorrows."

The screen went black. Knowing, austere murmurs ran through the crowd.

News reports flashed on the screen talking about the sudden disappearance of I-Ron. Headlines questioned his safety. Articles pinwheeled across discussing the possibility of abduction, maybe even (though nobody wanted to consider it) death. Screenshots of his barren feed came up. Headlist, JabberJaw, Picturebox, TimeWaster, Us-Stream— all of them had not seen activity in *six* hours.

The screen then changed and showed clips from around the world after it was announced formally by all news sources and those close to him that I-Ron was dead. Prime Minister Toshi Iwamoto had said it best, "It is like the soul has been ripped out of the world."

The movie continued. It cut to shots from the mourning that followed. In Beijing, citizens torched skyscrapers. In Lisbon, thousands drowned themselves in the Tagus. San Francisco: the Golden Gate bridge was bombed. Nairobi: people drove their cars at full speed into buildings. The grief was felt all over. Despair took hold. Cities burned, towns were obliterated, blood flowed from rooftops and along escalators; bodies lined the streets, as people warred in reverie.

"We take a moment," the narrator solemnised, "to remember and honour those who have transitioned to the Cloud."

Everyone bowed their heads as the casualty toll scrolled up on the screen:

> A Coruña – 1,200
>
> Aachen – 756
>
> Aarhaus – 9,012
>
> Abbeville – 2,159
>
> Aberdeen – 32,637

The list scrolled on and on at breakneck speed for three minutes before the screen faded to black once more.

The narrator then broke the silence: "He may have been gone. We may have been left in shadow. But only in darkness can you find the light."

The final image of the movie illuminated on billions of screens worldwide. It was a simple shot of @I-Ron_the_Eyecon's feed. A post from three days after the blackout that simply read:

What the hell happened? (posted 1 minute ago)

At the sight of this, the crowd erupted into applause, whooping and cheering, as the screens turned off and the lights went up. Shanta Lee wiped the tears from her eyes and blew her nose. She was never one for public displays of emotion, but given the circumstances, everyone was permitted a pardon.

"Everybody!" Shanta rejoiced, her cheeks red, shimmering under the light from dried tears. "With over four billion followers across all social media platforms, 750 billion views on Us-Stream, JabberJaw's most trending human being of all time; our saviour, and my personal hero, the greatest, the most high – *@I-Ron_the_Eyecon*!!!!"

I-Ron stepped out from the wings. The crowd went ballistic. A cacophonous roar shook the frame of the stage. Chants of "He is risen" rang out from the crowd. All the screens burst into life displaying images of I-Ron. Hands splayed, fists pumped, people reached out. All manner of projectiles were launched into the air. Everyone cheered—Shanta, the management team, the event techs, the crowd, the viewers at home: everyone. The applause and calls were so booming, so simultaneously widespread, that the moon tilted a further one degree on its axis.

I-Ron went to the mic stand. Shanta Lee fell to her knees and bowed her head to the ground. He stood there, bombarded by the rush of air that jetted forth from over three million rapturous voices.

A deafening shush rang out over the crowd, and after a few seconds, everyone fell silent.

I-Ron stood at the mic, staring out. He adjusted his tie-dye shirt and baseball cap, cleared his throat and spoke: "Err…hey…everyone."

"Aye, aye, guys," boomed the crowd.

I-Ron grimaced. "I…err…this seems a lot for just me."

"I LOVE YOU, I-RON!!" screamed Jim Cummings, who, like all of his office, had been given the day off to view the ceremony.

"I…err…love you too."

Jim Cummings screeched, his eyes rolled back into his head, and he fell backwards, dead, against the miasma of surrounding bodies.

"Why did you all do this?" asked I-Ron.

The crowd seemed confused.

"B-because you died," an Eyeconian called out.

"Then *rose* three days later," quickly added a pious I-Ronian. Her fellow I-Ronians patted her on the back for her speedy and accurate response.

"But I didn't die."

Many of the spectators laughed. He was so humble, so full of humility.

"You don't have to worry about us, I-Ron. We know the truth."

"So true," murmured some crowd members.

"No," stated I-Ron, "that is the truth."

"But you didn't post, I-Ron."

"I just turned off my phone."

Another pious I-Ronian followed suit to their members earlier nimble wittedness, "I-Ron Two-Eighteen—'I never go anywhere without my charger'."

Knowing '*ahhs*' rang out from the crowd.

"I didn't *die*," I-Ron affirmed. "I went to my private island."

"Yeah?" protested a crowd member, "if you went, who took you? What airline did you fly with?"

"I…well, I didn't have a pilot. I flew there myself."

"He flew!" hollered an Eyeconian.

"He can fly!" rejoiced an I-Ronian.

"PRAISE HIM! PRAISE HIM!" bellowed the crowd.

And with that they mobbed the stage. Millions rushed forward, slamming into each other. They broke through the metal barricade like toothpicks. They clambered over the edge, charged the stairs. Shanta Lee was trampled to death with the biggest smile on her face as she held onto I-Ron's leg.

I-Ron was swarmed. Hot, sweaty bodies engulfed him. All clamoured for a grasp, a touch, a graze of I-Ron. I-Ron batted away at their hands.

"Please I-Ron!"

"I love you, I-Ron!"

"HE IS RISEN!"

"You saved my life, I-Ron!"

"Let go me!" shouted I-Ron.

"I was in your first thousand followers, I-Ron!"

"Praise him!"

"I'm not special!" yelled I-Ron.

"You are He made flesh," proudly announced an I-Ronian as he stabbed an Eyeconian in the spine for a chance to grab I-Ron's t-shirt.

"I'm not!" I-Ron renounced.

"You died!"

"I didn't!"

"You can fly!"

"I CAN'T FLY!!" boomed I-Ron.

A beam of light suddenly shot down from the sky and fell on I-Ron. He looked up, his vision blurred by the light. I-Ron could feel his feet lifting. The crowd simmered. They gazed, open mouthed, their eyes following I-Ron's gradual ascent.

"Shit," he said as he floated up into the sky.

She Bleeds with the Fields by Gracious Love

The fields are streaked with red, but we cannot see this red. It screams the screeching song of a scarlet river invisible to the naked human eye. This screaming travels far and wide over the fluffy white taxis and bubblegum blue buses, but it falls on deaf ears. We are invisible to what we cannot hear and see. Humans do not hear the voices of nature screaming out in agony as trees crumble to the ground, roots twisting as they scramble to desperately hold the weight of the sinking ship. But people continue to hack, saw and spew smog in the air.

But she does not. No, rather she bleeds with these fields. These fields look at her as if she is a strange vegetable they have never known, because she bleeds with them. But her blood is visible to humans. Dark and metallic like copper coins with the texture of honey, splattering against leaves and leaving streaks on trees. She wheezes and she groans, but they cannot help her. They are but leaves, trees, grass and greens!

She crumples like a deflated balloon, the sickening thump of a body against mother nature's carpet of green causing a nearby crow to twitch his head up in confusion. He's a little thing, with a glossy coat that would make any female long to be his mate, if he weren't such a devious little creature, pinching with his tiny claws. There's an air of quiet smugness about him, even as he struts up to this girl, who appears to be clutching at her chest and whispering words to a series of green blades that have not the patience to care.

"Little thing," he squawked out, beating his wings as he scrambled to perch on her shoulder. Beady black eyes similar to a doll's eyes peer down at her with a mixture of amusement and curiosity.

She imagines him being a teenage boy with blackened lips and scruffy hair that is fluffy all the same. She imagines him as a teenager just like her, with his school uniform untucked and his blazer not ironed and his homework missing and his shoes unpolished. She wonders what kind of life he would've lived if he were without feathers and wings and sharp little claws.

"What brings you to my mother's fields?" The crow asks, and she knows that he doesn't speak of the mother that birthed his egg, but rather the mother that birthed this Earth with her bare hands.

"I have come to die," she wheezed. The words sound pathetic even to her, but the crow doesn't laugh, simpy cocks his head to the side, as if he doesn't believe her.

He chuffed. "Die, you say? I cannot understand why! Look around you, child. Look what our mother gave us. She gave us fields, waterfalls, oceans, volcanoes, trees, fruits, vegetables. *Life.* How darned ungrateful of you to throw it away."

He doesn't seem like a smug teenager anymore that smokes behind church and draws rude pictures on vans. He seems more like an old man, like her father, a ranch man. She pictures him, hands on his aging hips and a strand of straw in his mouth, a pristine Stetson on his head. Maybe he would even have a gun in a holster at his waist, maybe even a couple of knives in his boots. But she knows this is not his way. He attacks with words, not his claws.

She turns away from his judgemental stare, pressing trembling lips to the cold, green hills once more. "Go away. I ain't doing nothing wrong, you hear me? What's a girl gotta do to die in peace, huh?"

The smugness returns, and she sees him now, grey blazer creased as he pulls a lighter and a cigarette from his breast pocket as he shrugs. "I don't know. You humans have been coming onto these here fields for years now. Why won't you leave us alone? We ain't done nothing wrong."

She scowls at him, but he doesn't shrivel away. "You mind your own business! This Earth is our home too! We got a right to build and expand our community if we want to. You damn crows don't get no say in it, and it ain't like any gods have come down here to tell us off, so what harm is it? None, if you ask me."

He laughs, a great sound for a creature so small. "No harm, huh? You humans are stupid. Mother's been sending you signals all along. These fields are streaked with the blood of Mother's babies, but you don't care about their screams. No one does," he grumbled, and there's a dark expression on his face now as digs his nails into her cheek, all calmness gone.

"No, you don't care, you selfish beast. Nah, you just come here to suffocate these flowers and knolls with your greedy blood! Bathe us in it, why don't you? Won't make no difference. We're all dying anyway. All that smoke in this sky is gonna make you choke and choke and *die*. But what does it matter to you? You're already dead, little girl. Ain't no one gonna save you now," he snarled, all venom as claws snatched at her vunerable throat.

"Stop," she croaked, but he doesn't listen, and she almost doesn't want him to. Kindness—the mercy of another breath—would only crush her heart more than it already has been. "Damn crow, let go of me!"

He released her, paying her no mind as he continued to trudge up the hill, those unpolished shoes squeaking and squelching in the mind. She watches him go, spots still dancing in her vision as he sings a merry little tune over the breeze of a pixie's flute.

"Humans, humans, they ignore our cries," he sang gallantly, leaping over a cluster of mushrooms as he twirls with nature's orchestra. *"Let's let them suffer and die! Up above a breeze so high, a single pine cone twirls in the midnight sky. Humans, humans, scream and die, like you've cursed us so many times."*

The pool of blackness expands over her chest as the crow boy dances with an invisible partner, and she is helpless to sing along as she takes what she assumes will be her final breaths.

***

They aren't. She awakes what she assumes is hours later, a sticky substance on her chest. It's damp and smells like the calling of the rich, but she can't place what exactly it is. Sitting up, she notices that she is in a four poster bed, quiet voices murmuring nearby.

"She's unwell!" A voice hisses, a woman's. She sounds aghast, almost as if she can't believe what she is listening to.

"I don't care!" A man shouts back, the rattling of a teapot echoing after his shout. She hears the distinct sound of china breaking, but she is not familiar with china at all. How peculiar.

Seconds later, the door is turning, and in walks a couple that she has never seen before. There is a man dressed in a sapphire robe and white slippers. There are dark circles under his eyes and there is a frown on his face as he surveys her, his lip twitching as he turns away, probably disgusted at the sight of her.

The woman, on the other hand, is dressed in a pretty pink dress with identical heels and gloves to match. A necklace of diamonds rests against her cleavage, and in her arms is a tray, adorned with a china teapot and a plate of cucumber and butter sandwiches. She smiles warmly at her guest.

"Hello, dear," says the woman in pink. "How're you feeling now that we've mended that awful wound?"

"Crows," she says on instinct, and Mother must've been listening.

Whole flocks of the things gather on the window sills, all feathers with greedy black eyes and claws that can pick locks and choke people and claw their eyes out. She sees red each time another one crowds on the window sills, thumping against the glass and causing the couple to back away in alarm as the glass shakes and china breaks.

Then she sees him, one with his flock. His blackened lips are pulled back in a smirk, blood beneath his fingernails from where they'd clawed at her in places they weren't welcome. He opens his mouth and chants along that same song from before and she's helpless as she joins in.

"Humans, humans, they ignore our cries.

Let's let them suffer and die!

Up above a breeze so high,

A single pine cone twirls in the midnight sky.

Humans, humans, scream and die!

You've cursed us so, so many times.

Let's squash this child tonight."

A mass of feathers surge towards her as the crow boy

cackles, smoke rising into the air as a million beaks peck at every inch of her skin, claws pulling and ripping and scattering burgundy into the air and all over the bedsheets. She sees a single grave as he hovers over her dying corpse, sliding two silver dimes over her eyes, blocking the view of the grave that adorns her name: Annabelle Grey.

Sailboat by Jarrett Mazza

IT WILL FLOAT.

The boat, constructed from crumpled, scrunched paper, I sealed it with a fresh coat of wax. The current from the approaching storm, I believed, would help it to sail. Bending the paper, I made it when I was ten. I can still see my hand, gliding as I separated the four sections and curving each of the corners. The next step is to remake the triangle, yet the page, still ruffled and ripped in the corners, is flimsy, soft.

I shudder and I remember.

Too damn soft.

With the triangle section completed, I fold the bottoms and the sides and reshape the hull. Life, a flat circle, often it curves, disrupting symmetry, and what sinks, as I've come to know, can still be remade, can still *survive*. The process, though meticulous and somewhat *prosaic*, that is to make a boat out of paper, the purging of one's memories, however, is easier if the evasion is connected to something tangible.

The storm, torrential, I woke early to retrieve some old paper from a shelf by the window. My father believed work with your hands was the best work of all.

At the desk, my hands dropped, and I looked over and saw him as he walked by.

Look, I made a boat!

Shaking his head, he ran his hand across his sallow scalp and slammed his fists.

Sleeping!

The brushes and scissors jumped and, in midair, one of

the blades clipped my left eye. Head down, refolding the paper, I lathered it quietly in bed. The only sounds heard were those that could be detected if you were standing too close to the door.

Bent and sharp, the boat stayed in the desk and there it remained until the next storm.

If you're going to build something, build something that takes a long time to die.

Arguing with mother two days later, he threw a toolbox at her feet and shouted. The boat, stiff as a knife, I remembered waving it around as I ran outside. The rainfall made puddles of placid water and I stopped, kneeled, and splayed my fingers to gauge the temperature. Easing the boat into the stream, it skittered. Graceful, quivering, boats change with the current, and what's smooth one day can be rough the next, and such is only determined only by the intrepidness of its captain, the *will* of its maker.

Hard fists, loud voices, every parent is guilty of hitting their kids at least once or coming so close that, what forces them to go no further, is but a fragment of self-control; a little less of a violent temper compared to their counterparts. Children obey and obedience breeds honesty and honesty turns them into good, honest people; the kind of child that every parent wishes for their kids to grow up to be.

Children aren't born this way. Making them requires time, effort, and...

Unable to really communicate, or keep order, as father said, the next point of control is the easiest.

Hunkering by the stream now, the cold air gnawing at my neck, even today the boat feels hard as it did. Having creased the angles too much then, I had not let it go but swore today that I would, needed to. Father's hands, not chiefly created to preserve order, sometimes they were also used to lift and to hold things.

On Tuesdays, he would let me sit next to him and eat dinner in front of the TV.

As I hold the broken boat, old memories emerge in a cascade of opalescence. Every colour shows a different day. With a dark sky, listening to the trickling sounds of water, so soothing yet simultaneously inhibiting, I try to avoid any flashbacks. Kneeling, the boat's edges, crisp, and shelled in the wax that I had only haphazardly applied, it will be ready. Just waiting for more wind, a harsh breeze hopefully, and maybe some rain too, though *not too much* because it would sunder the vessel, diverging it from its course.

There was only one place it needed to go.

Fortuitous the entire act, and me, only willing to send it on a straight stream, a straight path that I could observe from beginning to end.

No child is raised without punishment and no parent should be unwilling not to deliver a swift one when necessary, and I thought that's what it was... *then*. Communication, negotiation, explanation and due diligence, the so-called modern-day parenting methods taught by those who labelled themselves as experts...they all say the same.

No one knows for sure what works. All made up as you go along.

The book of good parenting, a communal assembly of measly verbal exchanges and other untold stories, all passed down to those who are willing to tell their own tall tales while never disclosing the *actual* truths that credit them with *actual* experience.

Mythic, almost apotheosized because of their alleged

'goodness', the only good parent is the one who is not afraid of being a bad one.

At the time I made the boat, I found a kite in our garage. Twangy, its rope was thin and plaited. It scratched my hand as I pulled. It was given by mom who said she would help me fly it.

If not today, then another. I promise.

Unraveling a hunk of peeling string, I tied it to the base of the purple triangle. Sauntering down the steps, refusing to conceal the bonhomie, I listened to the wind, passed by the nearest window, stared at the unblemished sky. Searching, the kite was still dragging behind me. In the basement, I saw him; sprawled, feet hanging off the sofa, no shoes, wearing only one sock. He snored and a spillage of drool leaked from his gaping mouth. Nudging, the wind, transient, there was only so much time before the weather would change. Mumbling, his body smelled. I didn't know why he had chosen to sleep there. His bed was only a few steps away.

Shouting, he jolted, and his ability to stand futile. He was gone well before I found him. Smiling, lifting my hand to show him, it was on days like this where it would surely fly- getting so high I could pinch it between my fingers, like a coin.

Sleeping!

His yell, quick just like his hand, he whacked me with his pillow.

Often, parents choose to hold back their screams because often it's to not their intention to lose composure or to raise a hand. Avoiding pain, control is more than just a requirement, because pain is always what follows, but stability is the gift that is bestowed upon those deemed as strong-minded, the *unbreakable*.

Soft.

To reflect on childhood is to remember times of imparting wisdom; the procuring of either regret or relief. Never both. Even the best upbringings are peppered with a few absent moments, a long list of mistakes. To say that nothing bad ever happened is to insult the happiness received.

To define trauma, strenuous and chained by that which has happened but is not forgotten, such is not defined by the self or by others, and certainly not by those who claimed to have had it better; *those that say not everything was as good as it should have been.*

Exhaling, tendrils of mint-smelling smoke wafted near my face. I could only ask him so much before his vigor remerged.

Earnin' and burnin' was what he called work.

No time for softness. Time's a wastin'.

A fast reactor—the defining attribute of success—the words he chose sounded the same.

Do, don't just sit by and watch.

Considering his life, the details are buried in a long calumny describing the man that he only thinks he is, except it's not the false ideas or nefarious deeds I remember. Pity, because I knew his choices were burning him from inside. It's all true and yet, I can't think of anything that could be.

Why care to know now when he's gone.

Seeing him, another shudder followed by another moment of longing singes my nerves, I don't miss him. I just see him.

Ignited by the vicissitudes created after things deemed

too fragile to hold onto, maybe I *was* or *maybe* my preconceived notions about what it really means to raise a child will never be attained until I have one of my own.

The boat's edges, so sharp they nearly cut my skin, the folds, imperfect, they're not as symmetrical as I would have liked, but it will—*must*—float. The downpour, lighter, drops trickle the sidewalk and I'm standing in rubber boots, donning a pink poncho, with no umbrella, feeling the rain as I stand by and wait.

Stop!

Screaming, I hear nothing I haven't already.

Just more memories.

Hands up, magnanimous, I should have gone on, but then I am remembering the day when I asked about dinner.

Provoked, often it was just a word or a phrase that rocked his stability, always so delicately assembled. On a bad day, it's human to demand silence from the interminable world. A lonely man, scared, I knew, but if one does not try and eliminate the bad moments, they will turn calamitous, *ruthless* and there is no shell made for the human spirit that's capable of enduring. Only time heals, yet we are still perforated by the badness that festers in the moments that lie between.

Whatever happens, at least once, they'll float.

Pushing the chair, leaping, I feel fists—solid as oak— and see the food in his mouth seeping past his lips while the morsels trickle out like blood-soaked bits of bones, splurged together in a great vomit of gore. Through gritting teeth, I begged until an endless chain of hands sock me like waves crashing my sternum. I pretend I'm on a beach, and what I'm tasting is sand.

Twenty-eight, my father was twenty-two when he had

me, and was twenty-nine when she left. Older, I thought he was when he raised me, he did it the same as his father did, and his father before him.

Now there's only me.

I see a reel comprised of so many moments that I once thought were confounded to me for all time. Always, there's always the promise of absolution, and of order, and yet the real trauma lurks in the spaces between our most precious, frail seconds.

Every day a parent tries just a little more than theirs did.

Whatever their child asks for, they receive.

Feed me, help me, protect me.

And the parent gives. The child shouts. It whines. And all day long, their bleeding, querulous, perpetual begs persist—demanding more, more, *more*. Following the parent like an odor, what they crave is just a small sign that lets them know they were caring enough, wise enough, good enough. Then the whining returns, and the outcome of asking too much is fear and the cure for such? A hand, a kick, another scolding gesture that preserves order, keeps the peace.

A parent provides, a child takes, and everything is going to be okay.

Make sure there are no holes. All it takes is one for it to sink.

I will. A few holes isn't going to stop it.

Rainfall and thunder, it's only just beginning. The currents, rippling against the gutter, effervescing the intricacies of the narrow sidewalk, I hunker as I hold my own little precious tool of catharsis, of *succor* with both hands. The paper, still crinkled, still ripped, the wax manages to keep it, and the blue remains.

It's the same as the sky when it rains.

It's his as much as it is mine.

Opening my hand, I let it go, watching it skirr; a ship obdurately battling the wind, capitulating the current. It beleaguers and I ameliorate, and the memories ploddingly disappear—with the only fragments that remain the tiny drops in between—so small you can catch them all with only one hand.

Lord of the Feathers by Steve Goodlad

I spent many years as a humble priest in this backwater of Yorkshire and whilst my flock were honoured to have me as their reverend, I found the duties I performed somewhat misunderstood and overlooked. Ironically, I had begun my ministry with some vigour, trying to improve the lives of the local folk by campaigning to reduce licensing hours to three days a week and increasing the number of sermons I read. Sadly, the hostility this raised influenced my popularity within the community as well as at home where my wife declared me senseless which was a harsher reaction than the frosty glances of my public.

Eliza's lack of alliance with my ideas for community harmony was troubling, and I often looked in askance for the source of her displeasure with my work. In fact, on one such occasion I was watching her chop the logs from a great branch that she had dragged home. She knew I needed peace for several hours whilst I composed the sermon for Sunday communion, however she hacked and sawed for much of the afternoon until that branch was little more than a pile of logs. I knew she did not find living in Yorkshire easy, hailing from Burnley as she did. Fortunately, the distraction created by raising our seven children kept her occupied for a few years. Working part-time whilst doing so at the Plume of Feathers also gave her a distraction and some much-needed income as our parishioners were stereo-typically tight-fisted and lacking in charity.

I have little memory as to when it started, but her noble loyalty to my causes began to wane as the years rolled by and my career prospects flattened, whilst several curates had served the area and had gone to much larger parishes.

Hard, though I struggled to reassure Eliza that matters such as these were quite beyond my power and her poor understanding of the church hierarchy, she would raise the matter of my career over and over. Indeed, she even stopped me one day whilst mucking out the pig pen by beckoning me over. She'd heard that Reverend Kite in a neighbouring parish had become a Deacon after little more than three years as a vicar. Eliza knew full well that I could not risk getting my shoes dirty from the pig slew but still started to pitchfork the muck around with abandon even though the wheelbarrow was clearly full and required emptying. I was much troubled by her unhappiness and felt quite powerless to alleviate it since the demands of the parishioners had increased of late. Dorothy Hammond was hampered by melancholy following the demise of her cat Jeremy and I spent many an hour in her company trying to raise her spirits.

Over time I began to think that maybe I was being kept in Yorkshire for a reason, maybe a deeper quest than had yet occurred. I took to taking long walks so that my senses might be refreshed by the bracing Yorkshire wind. It never occurred to me that I might be walking upon the very answer to that question. I began beachcombing and taking home with me, pebbles whose colours delighted me and placing them on the mantelpiece. I was curious about them and I thought Eliza might share in my enthusiasm by joining me on my walks. However, when I found her, she was at the furnace, fashioning a new shoe for the dray horse. As she hammered away at the anvil making a terrible din, I put it to her that I had been thinking that my quest might have a deeper meaning than was being realised in this parish. I told her about the pebbles which had formed the basis of my thinking. She in turn told me that she had used them to construct a new rockery. I thought we did not have space for such ornamentation since the vegetables she grew supplemented our meagre income.

In the following argument I quite forgot how I had

started the conversation, completely losing my thread suggesting the compost heap she'd moved to accommodate the rockery could have been better used for the growing of potatoes. She threw the iron shoe back in to the furnace, pumped hard on the bellows to make the coals glow, and then removed the shoe white hot with the great clamps and shook it so near to my face I was nearly branded. Then she placed it again on the anvil and began hammering with such force the sparks fair flew.

Thankfully, I was not distracted from my walking activities and I also took a leap of purchasing a canvas knapsack and a small pick and all at once I became a man with a pastime that took me on journeys around the County and sometimes beyond. On one of these walks, I drifted into a town and noticed a little bookshop where I chanced upon a newly published volume on geology. What drove me to make such a rash purchase I will never know for it cost me most of the weekly stipend. Now Eliza would regret not planting more potatoes, I thought.

Further fortune ensued when on my way home, Eliza caught up with me on the Dray. She had been to the town to purchase more barrels of ale for the "Feathers". She naturally enquired as to my purpose in the town as we sat uncustomary next to each other. I enthused about my new pastime and I thought she listened intently despite her raucous singing at a volume even I with my sermon voice could not exceed, her baritone echoed in the forest around us and words I doubted even the inebriated patrons at The Feathers would tolerate.

She only stopped once we reached the Tavern. I had thought she could have dropped me closer to home. She jumped down and started to haul the barrels down off the cart and roll them into the cellar.

I did enquire as to when she thought dinner might be

ready and she stopped with a barrel held high above her head and looked so incredulous, perhaps because I had forgotten that on Wednesday's she worked from breakfast through to closing time. I mumbled an apology and set off towards home hoping at least for fresh dripping to go with the stale bread.

That evening, the children finally stopped trying to steal the last of the dripping when I got to read my new book. In the first chapter the geologist supposedly of some repute brazenly asserted that Silurian limestone was no less than one hundred thousand years old. This was despite the fact that the Bible tells us that the earth was created a mere six thousand years ago.

This was not mere error, this was deliberate slander, a poisonous assault on the good book. I was appalled. I am not without some academic intelligence of my own and I resolved to counter the half-baked thoughts that had crystallised into a strong counter argument and make it my mission to eradicate these heinous views from the so-called thinking academics, these atheists. I re-read Genesis:

'And a river departed from Eden to water the garden, and from there it divided and became four tributaries. The name of the first is Pishon, which is the circumnavigator of the land of Havilah where there is gold. And the gold of this land is good; there are bdellium and cornelian stone. And the name of the second river is Gihon, which is the circumnavigator of the land of Cush. And the name of the third is Chidekel, which is that which goes to the east of Ashur; and the fourth river is Phirath.'

More enlightened archaeologists place the congruence of these rivers in Persia, and if I could raise the funds to travel there, I felt sure with Gods will that I could provide substantial evidence to silence these heathens.

And that is when my thinking took a darker turn. I had no available funds but I knew I could acquire it. I would have to confess to Peter at the Pearly Gates when my time came for so odious was my proposed crime to acquire the necessary passage to Persia.

At the next full moon, I went to the church graveyard and I dug up Jeremy's grave and removed the diamond encrusted collar he had been buried in. As I stepped from the hole, my cassock fell over my head as I was reaching out for a hold. I heard a shriek and stood frozen for several moments thinking I'd been rumbled. When I removed the cassock, I spotted old Mrs. Hubbard lying on her back by the perimeter fence mumbling incoherently about ghosts. She clearly required urgent help, so I filled in the hole, returned the stone over the grave and about an hour later I carried Mrs. Hubbard to Doctor James house and he quickly took on the task of assessing her mental faculties whilst I scurried home hoping to arrive before Eliza arrived back.

The next day, I prised the diamonds from the collar and placed them inside a velvet purse and buried the collar good and deep under the rockery.

At my next sermon I announced my intention to sail from Whitby to Tilbury and from there to charter a ship to Persia. I would need a butler, servants and a maid and possibly a navigator and I pleaded benevolence from my flock. All six of them stared in awe as I stood in the pulpit. Even Eliza looked stunned.

When I returned home, Eliza confronted me by the hearth where I was hoping for much needed warmth. I told her about the book and my intention to dispute the authors claim and reinforce the argument made by the scriptures by travelling to Persia. I told her that I had a small heirloom, as in the diamonds that I intended to cash in and buy my passage.

She cut me down like a scythe. I swear I have never felt such degradation. I was on the cusp of my mission in life to prove the scriptures to rid the planets population of these ridiculous notions that the earth existed, indeed was inhabited long before the scriptures say it was. The half-formed thoughts that had crystallised into a strong counter argument and become my mission to eradicate these heinous views from the so-called thinking academics, these atheists, and before I could even reach my own hearth my wife, a mere woman was preventing me.

"Listen," she said as she sat heavily on my chest.

"Poppet?" I croaked.

"I feel no bitterness, I cast no blame." With every word she bellowed, my head bounced off the flagstones. "I married an idiot, and must accept equal culpability. You may valiantly preserve your faith, but I have a greater design of my own for you. I have waited years for the smallest sign and I have received it, just now in that purse. I require your full commitment as I have committed to your fruitless career for many a long year."

I could barely breathe; there was no hope of equalling such resounding determination even from my pulpit.

"Eden is in this fair County, even I accept that now and it has been waiting to be revealed to us given the right circumstance. This is what your flock needs," she said with a prophetic air. "I would not be so gently persuasive as I am right now if I did not believe you and I could meet it with success. So, you have before you, next Sunday's sermon, your last in this parish, for you, my woeful husband, are going to finally be of use. Your 'heirloom' will enable me to buy The Feathers. I am giving you the promotion you always desired. You will of course have lord in your title: Landlord of The Plume of Feathers."

Moustachio by Laura Scotland

The light in Nora's stairwell was out. She fumbled blindly for her keys but they slipped from her fingers and fell to the floor with a deadened clink.

"Fuck," she grumbled, then knelt down to grope the damp, gritty concrete.

Kyran opened the door. He yanked it dramatically then leaned against the frame looking down at his friend in bemusement.

"Light's out again," he remarked, then took a sip from the pink cocktail he'd been cradling against his chest. Nora snatched up her keys and rose to her feet. Her back ached. She wondered if the eyeliner Kyran was wearing was hers. Making a face, she pulled the drink from his hand and downed it as she swept past into their shared flat.

"Hey! That was the last of my gin!" he remarked, ruefully accepting the empty glass from her outstretched hand.

"Your gin?" Nora asked, over her shoulder.

"Okay, *your gin*," he mumbled.

Nora kicked off her shoes and threw herself down on the sofa while Kyran disappeared into the kitchen and began clanking bottles and glasses. When he emerged it was with two frothy cosmopolitans garnished with delicate twists of orange peel. Nora accepted the cocktail gratefully, breathing in the sharp scent of zest as she took a drink. There were perks to having a bartender for a flatmate.

"Tough day?" Kyran asked.

"You have no idea." Nora put her glass down to rub her eyes. "Tom is such an asshole. His asshole has an asshole, that's how much of an asshole he is. And the only people he promotes are assholes."

"Is he the one you have your meeting with?"

"Yes. Tomorrow." Nora sighed. She plucked at a snag on the knee of her tights. "Though I don't know why I've bothered to arrange it. I can't even ask for a day's holiday without st-st-stuttering apologetically. I am so fucking pathetic."

Kyran lifted one of his sculpted brows. "Because you're not an asshole?" He paused for a moment and his expression softened, then he reached into his pocket and pulled out a little box tied with a black ribbon. He put it on the table next to Nora's glass.

"What's this?" she asked.

"Just a little good luck gift."

Nora eyed her friend suspiciously, but he laughed and raised his palms.

"No joke! I'm being perfectly serious. I remembered about your promotion meeting, that's all. And these..." he tapped the little box, "are meant to work really well. Guaranteed success. Go on, open it!"

Nora regarded the box for another moment, then plucked it from the table and pulled the ribbon. Inside, on a bed of tissue paper, she saw what appeared to be a small moustache. The strands were thick and glossy, neatly trimmed, and long enough at either end to form two elegant curls. She stared at it, then removed it from the box and held it up, feeling thoroughly bewildered.

Kyran grinned. He rose to his feet, unable to contain his excitement. "It's a Moustachio! They are *all the rage!* My mate Peter bought one last week and he's like a new man! Confident, dignified, cracking jokes over the bar and winking at cute girls—he went on three dates last weekend! Peter!"

Nora glanced up, incredulous. "Bad-breath Peter?"

"Bad-breath Peter! Three dates. I'm telling you, if you're looking for confidence, this is the thing." Kyran sat down next to Nora and gently took the moustache from her hand. He fitted it to her upper lip with solemn concentration, then smoothed the curls and pulled his hands away with a smile.

"Voila!"

Nora let out a glib laugh, but as she touched the moustache, gingerly stroking it with her fingertips, her mirth faded. It fitted perfectly. She rose, spilling her cosmopolitan, and darted to the hall mirror. What she saw there was startling. The moustache changed her entire face, accentuating her cheekbones and the small pink bulge of her lower lip. Its fine strands were the exact shade of russet as the hair on her head, and her usually plain brown eyes seemed livelier, newly flecked with shards of gold. Something about her new reflection caused her to raise her chin. The moustache itself was very comfortable. Instead of feeling itchy or rough, it was silky, soft, and warm. She twitched her mouth, trying it out, finding its range of expressions enormously pleasing. Her eyes flitted to Kyran who was standing behind her, waiting. When their eyes met a flush began to spread across Nora's cheeks.

"And I'm meant to wear it..."

"Whenever you want! They're quite secure, according to Peter. Apparently he wears his *all the time*, if you know what I mean. Swears by it."

Nora's cheeks were burning. The thought of showing up to work with a moustache was equally terrifying and thrilling. Her colleagues might whisper. Some would laugh.

But the longer she stared at her reflection the more she felt as if the joke would be on them. Wearing this she could imagine herself looking Tom in the eye. She looked at Kyran again, still fighting the last shreds of uncertainty.

"Do you think I can pull it off? I mean, it's not really my kind of thing."

Kyran tilted his head back and let out an exasperated groan. Then he reached out and grabbed Nora by the hand, pulled her into hold, and then began waltzing her around the room, hopping over the discarded shoes and empty spirits bottles in their path.

"*Make it* your kind of thing!" he cried, spinning her and then letting go with a flourish. Nora shrieked with dizzy laughter as she stumbled and regained her balance, back where she'd started in front of the mirror. She gazed at her reflection as she caught her breath. The moustache was like a fine brushstroke, a finishing touch that made her to push her shoulders back and stand taller than before. She smoothed the tiny curls, then turned to her friend, eyes shining.

"I love it!"

My Girlfriend's Plants by Robert Scott

My girlfriend loves Twitter, Facebook and chatting on the phone, but her real-world physical friends are her houseplants; all thirty-two of them. So, that leaves me sharing a one-bedroom flat with Rosa and her thirty-two pals.

Of course, living in a world of concrete, in a city-centre flat, the indoor greenery is great. I get that. But with each springtime burst of growth, I wonder, how big are they are going to get. Will there still be room for me? They could kick me out one day.

Lately, I have tried to be more friendly. Making an effort to get on with your partner's social circle seems the right thing to do; even if you don't all end up as firm friends, and even if they are plants.

Very soon, I will need to take the relationship to the next level. Rosa is flying home this afternoon. For the next ten days I will be chief carer and companion to all, from the tiny scraggy beansprout things in yogurt pots under the kitchen sink to the six-foot high big guy in the living room.

Unfortunately, this news has come at short notice. After a year of lockdown, governments have decided to allow us more flights and bigger social bubbles. Since Rosa got her ticket, she has been busy packing and planning her trip. In the rush of her preparations, my training as plant-sitter has been patchy, sporadic and rather tetchy at times, to be honest. Rosa thinks I should know more than I do as I have lived with these guys for three years. She has a point. I have watched many of them grow up and known a few since they were seeds.

The worry is that my upcoming plant-sitting challenge isn't only about the botanical side of things. It could well be a relationship test.

After three years together, we have never properly discussed marriage or children. Larger concepts loom. Responsibility. Reliability. Commitment. If I get it together to look after this lot while Rosa is away, do I pass? Is that what she is thinking? I could ask, but there doesn't seem time and I am not sure asking would help.

I am not wholly confident I will pass. I fear that these ten days will resemble those times I am left alone with a baby or toddler; when I know and they know that I am clueless about what to do, but we manage to share the vibe that it is a temporary situation and we will get through it if we play it cool.

When Rosa realized she had twenty-four hours to train me up, she started teaching me their names. When the Latin ones proved too much, she switched to the funny everyday ones, building on what I already call them: the 'Purple Orchid', 'Hello Vera', the 'Big Lad in the Living Room' and so on.

The foody ones are, of course, the simplest to identify—such as the little pots in the kitchen windowsill. Three bonsai trees, with two dozen tiny red chilli peppers scattered over them, the actual size of the menu pictures that tell you how hot a dish is. I suppose they have bigger versions in Mexico or India; given their large populations; they would have to. Our three sit there like miniature Christmas trees with their bright lights on all year, day and night.

Alas, such easy-to-spot foody ones are rare beasts in Rosa's jungle. The remainder are pretty much indistinguishable to me and boast nothing more to go on than the varying sizes and shapes of their green leaves— yes, all green—not even colour-coded! I realise there will be more subtle clues to decipher; that is what I need to learn.

It is not that I have no interest in plants; far from it.

At the start of Lockdown, for a laugh, I bought 'The Day of the Triffids' from my local second-hand bookstore. I gave up after twenty pages. It was way too scary for bedtime reading during those first few days when my Edinburgh city centre street—usually thronging with students and tourists—emptied and transformed into a post-apocalyptic movie set, with Rona-zombies hiding behind every corner. The bookseller snorted a dark, ironic chuckle at the sight of the old cover. His place has been closed for a year now. I hope the old boy is all right.

But that story does make you think. When we started to crawl out of the water, there were just a few of us, but billions of them. Poor bastards. They didn't see us coming. They must be pissed off with what we have done to their garden.

With hours to go before Rosa's departure, I still haven't learned the names of the thirty-two potted ancestors of those early days, so she labels them with blue post-it notes—names and numbers. Desperate measures. She writes down instructions. I should water 1, 4, 7 and 8 once a week (Saturday), and so on. More worryingly, for some she notes: 'when they need it'.

As I help her into the taxi with all her luggage, her last words are: "Text me if you're worried about any of the plants, any time."

For a second, I think she is going to give me a burner phone.

I wave goodbye and climb the stairs.

I slump on the sofa and send Rosa a text.

Looking up from the phone, I am met with a sea of

green. They suddenly appear so alive, especially so, right now, in my northern hemisphere April. They are vibrant, full of it. More so than a few of my old colleagues at the office, from what I remember. They even look happy. They don't know Rosa has gone and they are left alone with me for ten days.

It is as if they know I am here. Though not actually looking at me—they are aware of my presence. I wonder what they will make of being stuck with me. Will they miss Rosa? Will they blame me?

***

For the first few days, I miss Rosa too much to worry about the plants, although with working from home, I sit and move amongst them all day. They are no more than pieces of furniture. The home-working runs nine-to-five. Rosa texts me all day and phones or video-calls in the evening. She is seeing her friends and family, and is fully occupied, excited; there is a touch of stress too in her voice.

Mostly, the flat is so quiet. Plants don't make noises, I discover.

After a couple of days and prompted by Rosa's reminders, I walk around and check off the numbers on the pots, noting that I must keep an eye on a couple of them every morning, according to the instructions.

After that inventory, I notice them more. They begin to be a comforting presence; a connection with Rosa, who texts a little less often each day. Fair enough. She has waited a whole year to see her family and friends.

On Day Four, during a boring meeting, I see that the orchid on the fireplace has come alive—three buds have flowered into pinky-purple rosettes, the size of November paper poppies. When the meeting ends, I get the computer off my lap and go over. There are two more buds still to pop, just hanging out there, on a limb, ready to go. I will have to watch out for that.

Visiting and saying hello to the plants becomes my new breaktime pastime, a replacement for Rosa's regular texts. I tentatively touch and try to talk to them. I don't have Rosa's knack. She strokes the leaves as if they were the hands of an elderly relative in hospital.

When she talks to them, it is not gibbering baby talk—she listens to them, has conversations. She reads their moods. 'Ooh, what's wrong with you today?', 'Cheer up,' 'Let's get you a drink', 'Someone needs some love', 'What's wrong with you today, Little One?' As she wanders about, absorbed, she often leans over me to reach one with a water bottle, so I feel like Bruce Willis in Sixth Sense.

One funny thing I notice on Day Six is that when I am on the way to the shops, out for a run, or taking the rubbish out, I have started to check out the leaves on the trees and the greenery of the bushes. It reminds me of home and my responsibilities.

I begin to worry about 8, 5 and 21. They don't look right. Too much water? Not enough water? Further developing concerns are little bugs, patches of yellow, dried leaves in the base of pots. I don't want to trouble Rosa. I Google, but there are too many *unknowables* and *unfathomables*.

By Day Seven I feel I am losing a battle.

I wake up at 2.34. They are calling me. I go through to the living room. As I switch on the light, there is a Toy Story moment as they all get back in their pots and usual places.

I blink.

Next, it is like I am in a hideout cannabis factory. I feel the danger. I am intruding, crossing the line. This is not my space right now. Crazy urban paranoia. Triffid thinking. I grew up in a village. I have got this.

I put the light off and go back to bed. I wish Rosa will come back soon. She will be sleeping in her old room, after eating the food of her childhood.

The next day is a good day. Saturday. The plants seem to know it is the weekend. A time to hang out, spend some quality time.

I notice some of them are dusty. Who knew that happened? I clean them up, just wiping them with a wet kitchen roll. I hope that is the right thing to do. The rubbery ones enjoy it. I am extra careful with the fragile ones. They have all got to feel better after that.

I go out to buy some spray stuff to get rid of the bugs. I think of taking one of the little guys with me to cheer him up but leave it. When I come back, I see the final purple orchid has come out. I take a beautiful photo and send it to Rosa.

At six o'clock I put my feet up and have a drink. The room looks fantastic. I couldn't imagine the place without these guys. First, we learnt to rub along and survive, then more. They are all right, I like them—in the daytime anyway. I see more why Rosa loves them.

The phone goes. I tell Rosa about my day and scan the room to show her. She waves. They wave back. When she comes back to me on the screen, she is almost teary for a moment.

"You'll see them again soon," I say. "Just two more days."

"Oh, Al," she starts, as if she wants to tell me something. She bites her lip. "I'll call tomorrow. Same time."

She does call, as she said she would. And she does have something to tell me. I was right.

The first line is: "I'm sorry, Al. I'm not coming back tomorrow. Or ever." I have no words. I just look around the room. "You must have known, Al."

"Yes, I knew," I say, though I didn't.

She explains that her high school sweetheart recently broke off his engagement and now he and Rosa are back together.

I was wrong about the plant-sitting being the test. I had failed before Rosa left, at some point over the past three years. Rosa just didn't tell me the results before she left.

"We'll be all right, Rosa. Goodbye and thank you."

"Sorry? We? Thank you?"

"Thanks for the plants."

Private View by Steve Gregory

And when you finally realise that we are dickheads, and not the reasonable people you had chosen to believe, you will have only yourself to blame; yourself, and the fecundity of your misdirected imagination.

When you eventually ask us to leave, we will grab coats which may or may not be ours, and wine that definitely isn't. We will march out of the gallery like a band of victorious goblins, held together by a variety of toxins and a temporarily suspended mutual loathing.

Then, for us, the question will begin to remain: Whatever to do next?

For the night is yet young, whilst our potential sins are ancient. The volume of the blackish heavens above displays the vast capacity of the here-now for gleeful misdeeds.

So again: What to do?

More of the same. Much more. More than we could possibly remember on any possible morrow.

Perhaps we will do the sensible thing and proceed by drinking the pilfered wine. Or perhaps we will use it to decorate the nearest bus-shelter with our approximation of your work. Perhaps we will merely spill it on ourselves as another of our pointless debates inevitably turns bad-natured. Our favourite thing about small galleries is that the visibility through open-facade windows works in both directions. Quite a show indeed.

When the time comes that we feel we have proved whatever our weird point might be, or that we get bored of the hilarious pretence of disinterest on the faces of your fleeting friends, or that we simply forget what we're doing, than we will go:

Onwards, downwards, sideways; every which way but home

We will trawl a series of ever decreasing possibilities through this tawdry citadel, smirking all the way, heartened by the vocalisations of high hos. Then gradually, subliminally, we will disperse into the night like an obnoxious gas. We will roll, stoned and alone, privately stepping our addled vectors, for entropy beckons.

Severe and severally, we will waft into the foyers of our respective temporary dwellings. We will barely acknowledge the approximation of smile on the face-area of the uncanny welcome-bot, as we shuffle past like a bad apology, and head up the polypropylene hill to oblivionshire. We will shout at our plastic rectangles until the little fools allow us passage into our replicant cubicles.

Once interred, we will shed our night-shot fabric skins, and briefly squint through a hundred hazy channels, languorously hunting for some youngflesh epiphany.

At last, unsated but spent, we will curl ourselves up amongst strange textiles, and sleep the long, dark sleep of the damned.

∞

Why?

Why would you want to invite us to your little show?

Perchance, when you first saw us, cackling in the restaurant, our irreverence suggested a relentless joie-de-vivre. Perhaps our dilapidated charm reminded you of some characterful European farmhouse conversion; when, in truth, we more closely resemble a series of vile, crumbling outhouses. We never made any claims as to our nature: you simply liked the cut of our gibberish, and extrapolated from there.

And us, why would we accept such an invitation?

Well, this has happened before and it will happen again. The thought of young strangers and free wine makes us lick our internal lips, like secret vampires left to supervise the sleepover.

And what did you imagine would happen?

Did you think we would whirl in, tell you we love your work, and introduce you to powerful friends, whisking you stratospherically to new echelons of perceived success?

I almost pity you.

And in turn, perhaps you presume to pity us our malignancy. But think on this: Your empathy will be wasted, for we successfully stunted our emotions many years ago. The only tears we will ever excrete will be accompanied by raucous squawks, and tablethumping.

Or even, when all is irreparably done, you may attempt to bolster your psychology by believing that our cabaret of misanthropology was designed in some way for your benefit, to teach you a valuable lesson. Perhaps it would be this: In future, when inviting people to see your shitty little pieces, don't punch above your fucking weight, love. Go back to your loathsome flat and whittle your impossible fancies into shards of achievability.

Or do not. For truly, my dear, we do not give a fuck.

So now, right now, right here, in this preposterous restaurant, think hard little one, for the question is this:

Do you really want us to come to your show?

Because we fucking well will, my dear,

we fucking well will.

4.9 Stars by Joe Howsin

Rodney: EXCEPTIONAL: Great situation, host was excellent, good parking.

Sue: COMFORTABLE: Relaxed feeling to the place. Within walking distance of the town centre. Host provided everything we needed.

Janet: EXCELLENT: Excellent service.

Helen: MEMORABLE: Everything was exceptional. Other rooms elsewhere not of the same quality.

Matthew: SUPERB: Great room. Particularly pleasant given the odd circumstances we arrived in. Host sorted us all out. Intermittent Wi-Fi only allowed us to enjoy the room more.

Malcom: VERY GOOD: Very nice room, bathroom, kitchen area. Noise of nearby lift soothed us to sleep nicely.

Carmelo: GOOD HOTEL: Poor phone reception provided us much needed peace.

Peter: GREAT TIME: High price ensured quality.

John: SECURITY: Door not shutting properly at night

made us feel safer, knew host could reach us quickly if we were in trouble.

Jamie: EXCELLENT THROUGHOUT: Location is excellent. Close to beautiful fast river. Far from noisy traffic and pedestrians. Definitely stay here.

Rodney: LOVELY TREAT: Great deal. Couldn't stay long enough.

Alice: FOREVER: Would stay for longer!

Charlotte: LOVELY STAFF: Host was a joy, reassuring but not intrusive or overwhelming. Thoughtful changes to the place such as not servicing rooms. Room was sealed when I arrived. Host was so friendly and helpful.

Sheryl: OKAY: I'm here for a long term stay, five nights. Room is pleasant, but a little on the small side, and the blinds are difficult to close. Not seen the host yet, has anyone else had problems like this?

Calvin @ Sheryl: Nope! We found the room perfect size, blinds work perfectly, host was perfect, always there for us.

Sheryl: STRANGE: The door to my room was stuck for a few hours this afternoon and I couldn't get out, I missed out on having drinks with my friend. I called the number provided but I can't get hold of the host, can anyone here help?

SUSAN @ Sheryl: That is strange. Why would you go out for drinks? Complementary beverages in the fridge. Room fully vintage, door an original piece! Would love to be back there.

Furnell: GOREGOUS LUXURY ROOM: Loved the super king bed, shower good, all very comfortable, best part is location, very private space, no outside noise.

Sheryl: BLINDS: The door seems fine now, but the blinds are broken. Every night I close them before I go to bed, and every morning they're wide open. The sunrise wakes me up! Is there an electric motor that lifts them automatically? I still haven't heard from or met the host of the property. Has anyone else had this issue? P.S. I know it sounds silly, but I'm sure the room has gotten smaller?

Alice @ Sheryl: Sounds like you're the forgetful type. Blinds worked perfectly during my stay. Everything in the room is vintage. Very good quality fixtures.

Mark: PERFECT: Wonderful stay in old hotel. Great time, lovely room, helpful host.

Sheryl: SOMETHING'S NOT RIGHT: I definitely, *definitely* closed the blinds last night. I tied the cord tight so they couldn't be moved. Something woke me up early this morning and I saw that they were wide open!!! Worst of all I still haven't heard from the host! Can someone please contact him if you have an alternate number? The coat rack fell over today; the room seems tiny even compared to when I first arrived.

Helen @ Sheryl: Obviously can't tie a knot. Blinds were working perfect for me. Coat must've been too heavy for rack. Hope you didn't harm the room.

Sheryl: TERRIBLE PLACE: Last night will be my last in this place. I didn't bother trying to close the blinds. Woke up in the night and saw someone standing at the window. Whoever it was noticed I was awake and ran out of the room. When I tried to follow the door stuck again and I couldn't get out. Rang police but they took forty minutes. Didn't find anyone. STILL haven't seen the host!

Rodney @ Sheryl: WASTER. Clearly trying to get a discount. You'll see the host soon.

Sheryl: HELP ME: I can't get out. I was supposed to leave yesterday, but the wall has swallowed the door. Room seems so small and I can't breathe. Man stood against the window again last night, and we stared at each other until I fell asleep again. What is happening? Somebody please help.

Sue @ Sheryl: You're so lucky! Won't be long now, hope you enjoy your stay! ☺

Sheryl: HELP: He is in the room with me. I can't get out. I can't see him but he must be so close to me. I can't call the police, I can't call anyone. My phone won't close this hotel app. I can't get out. Please help me help me he

Arnold: SO NICE: Spacious, good location, quiet.

Samantha: GREAT VALUE: Clean bathroom and kitchen area, complimentary tea.

David: YES: Very good room! Will be returning soon.

Sheryl: FANTASTIC: Wonderful place, roomy, excellent fixtures, host was wonderful and always with me. Shower good.

Mrs. Bowley Upstairs by Ed Walsh

I was recently reminded of Mrs. Bowley. I hadn't thought of her in a long while, but maybe I'd seen someone who brought her to mind, or maybe had a similar voice, quite low and refined in the northern way. She lived above us at thirty-two Osanna Street. We had moved there from the south and had never been in the city before; had never been so far north in fact, not by a long way. We were on the middle floor; Mrs. Bowley was above. Although we could hear movement in the upstairs apartment, it wasn't until about six weeks later that we actually saw her. Or to be more accurate, Sybille saw her—that's Sybille, who was my wife then.

We came to the city because we thought we would be happy there, and that I would sell my paintings. But the nearest I had got to success in that line was working as night-security at the Tallentorf Gallery. *I* never doubted how good I was, but by that time I was coming to accept that I might be in a minority. Plus, we had a kid to raise— Danno, who was then about six—so I had to do whatever was necessary until someone with taste decided to give me a hand up.

One afternoon I was in bed after my shift when Sybille got to talking with Mrs. Bowley on the landing. After a few more such meetings she invited her in for coffee. I was in bed when this happened too, so didn't meet her that first time. But Sybille told me about her. Apparently she had been an actress, not famous but good enough to make a living in the forties and fifties. It seems she stopped acting and devoted herself to her husband after they got married. They had no kids, and had lived in the upstairs apartment all their married life. He, Alfred, had been a professor of literature at the Goyalca Institute but had been bed-ridden with some undiagnosed ailment for the past seven years.

"Except for the bathroom, its wall-to-wall books up there," she had said. Mrs. Bowley must have been about seventy when she was saying these things.

After a few weeks I got to meet her. She and Sybille were having coffee in our main room when I came through.

"Oh, Mr. Doles," she said. "It's so good to meet you at last. Sybille has told me so much about your work. I'm a great art lover myself. Not an expert by any means. I leave the expertise to Alfred. He specialises in the renaissance. He's fluent in Italian. You speak Italian, Mr. Doles?"

I said, "Not Italian, no," leaving open the possibility that I spoke other languages.

I hadn't realised they were on first-name terms—Sybille called her Madeleine. And Madeleine was what you might term a handsome woman. She did not try to disguise her age, but she clearly cared about the way she presented herself; everything she wore looked expensive and somehow mattered. She looked like how I imagined Sybille might look at that age, and that was nothing to fear. She also had a confidence which seemed unusual for someone who was in someone else's apartment, as if it was her apartment and I was the visitor. She told me that her husband would love to meet me, to talk about the arts and suchlike. Sybille knew I would hate that, but she said, "Wonderful. Wouldn't that be wonderful, Sorley, if the four of us could get together?"

"You'll have to come up when he's feeling well enough," Mrs. Bowley said. "Alfred's a great cook. It's just that he doesn't like the thought of anyone else in the apartment at the minute, with him being stuck in his bed. It's his pride, I suppose."

"Of course," I said, hoping that I didn't look too

relieved. "It's entirely understandable."

"But soon, hopefully, fingers crossed."

It must have been about four months after she first came into our apartment that Mrs. Bowley took to sitting in with Danno on Saturday nights so we could go out. It was her suggestion. She asked and we said yes. Luckily, Danno took to her and he also called her Madeleine. For some reason, I couldn't bring myself to do that even when I got to know her, she seemed too remote for that kind of familiarity. So to me, if I had to make any reference, she was Mrs. Bowley. And when she came down on Saturdays, she was more casual but still expensive. And she and Danno read, and watched TV, and she taught him to play chess, a game neither me nor Sybille had ever played.

On the first couple of occasions, Sybille asked if she was quite sure about the arrangement, and whether Mr. Bowley didn't mind. But she said that she had left him with his books and his whisky and he was fine. "To tell the truth, I think he's glad of a break from me. He never sees anyone else, not since his brother died, he was the only visitor."

We went to an Italian place a few streets away and were always back before eleven. Danno was always in bed by then; he was obviously more compliant with Mrs. Bowley than he was with us. And after a few minutes chat, she would go back up to her apartment and we would hear her moving about, tending to her husband.

It was a nice routine and in its way helped settle us into the city, because there was no doubt we were struggling to adjust before we had our night out. It helped to have a regular place to go to, a place where we were recognised and greeted.

About a year into this arrangement, we were ready to go out as usual. Danno had had a bath and had his pyjamas on. But, come seven-fifteen, Mrs. Bowley hadn't arrived.

"She must be busy with Alfred," Sybille said. "Give her ten minutes." But after ten minutes she hadn't come down, so I went up. I knocked gently and said her name, conscious of the echo on the landing. I assumed that at least one of them would hear me. The door wasn't locked, so I opened it a crack and said her name again.

Nothing.

I made my way along the passageway, calling her name. I could hear a TV. I knocked on the next door and then opened it. It was a large room, and that was where the sound was coming from. It was a quiz-show, one of those where people compete against each other to win a car or a holiday. I wouldn't have imagined Mrs. Bowley watching that kind of thing. The room was solidly furnished, dark and old-fashioned, and there was a man's suit hanging from the curtain-rail. It looked recently returned from the launderers. I thought of the abandoned ship, but couldn't recall its name. Then from behind I saw her hand on the armrest of a chair which was facing the TV. I guessed she had fallen asleep.

I said her name again, and as I walked round the chair the reason she had not been replying became apparent - she was dead. I had not seen a dead person before then, nor since. I don't know why, but after staring at her a while I said her name; I didn't say Mrs. Bowley, I said Madeleine, it seemed more intimate; the whole situation seemed *intimate,* and I wanted to touch her hair, but didn't. Then I remembered her husband. He must be lying there, unaware that his wife was dead a short distance from him.

"Mr. Bowley," I called. There was no noise except for the whoops from the quiz-show audience. It then occurred to me that she might not have been watching the quiz show, but that it might have started after she expired.

"Mr. Bowley, it's Sorley Doles, your neighbour from downstairs." I knocked on the only other door in the room, then I opened it. It was their bedroom, but Mr. Bowley was not in the bed. There were two bathrooms off. His was the tidier: shaving brushes and soaps neatly lined up on the small shelf above the basin, one large hairbrush, one small; scissors for nasal hair. Hers had her stuff scattered about and I didn't like to look too long. They had their own monographed towels—*AB* and *MB*.

I tried the other doors off the passageway. In one they kept their equipment, vacuum, ironing-board, the like; the other nothing, just an empty room with a radiator. I called his name again but it was pretty clear he wasn't in the apartment. Maybe we had misunderstood her, or maybe she had been exaggerating when she said he was bedridden. Either way, he must have gone out.

I went back into the front room and switched the TV off, then I looked at her for a long while. If this was what death looked like, it didn't look much to fear. She was ready for a quiet night in with Danno. She even made the effort for that. Her finger and toe nails were painted blue, and she was wearing one of the patterned scarves that she wore for style rather than warmth. As I was acclimatising myself to the silence, there was a knock on the outside door, then Sybille's voice: "Sorley, you in there?"

"He's not here," I shouted.

She came through and surveyed the room.

"Who's not here?"

"And she's dead."

"What?"

"Madeleine. She seems to be dead. *Is* dead."

"What?"

"Here." I pointed to her body.

"Are you sure?" She came round and saw that what I said was true.

"She was watching a quiz. And he's not here."

"Where is he?"

"How should I know?"

"My God. What do we do?"

"I don't know. Tell someone? The authorities?"

"Who are the authorities?"

"Not sure."

"Where are all the books?"

I hadn't noticed that, no books.

I went down and got the number for the caretaker, Dromond. I didn't say anything to Danno.

"It happens," Dromond said when he came. "I look after thirty apartments. People are sometimes there for weeks before anybody notices, older people mainly, by themselves. Sad, but there we have it."

"But she wasn't by herself. Her husband lives here. We don't know where he is."

"Husband?"

"Her husband, Alfred."

"Alfred? *Alfred?* No, I've been looking after these apartments nearly forty years. Mrs. Bowley has no husband. There's no Alfred. No husband Alfred anyway."

"No husband Alfred? That can't be right. I'm sure we've heard him moving around. We've heard her talking to him."

"Well, I don't want to contradict you good people, but Mrs. Bowley was born in this apartment, lived here with her mother until her mother died. And that was what - twenty, twenty-five years ago? By herself since. I've been in here a few times, repairs and suchlike, there's no husband. Nice woman though, always had a little something for me at Christmas."

"We must have heard wrong," I said.

When we went back down, Sybille said, "We didn't hear wrong." I said I knew that. That night, and for many nights after, we could hardly sleep. We would just repeat things that Madeleine had said, things which weren't true, or not true in any way that we understood true to mean. And we would try to work it all out. We came up with many explanations but couldn't settle on anything.

Dromond made the arrangements, and the three of us drove through the city and out to the crematorium with her. It was us and the priest. We sang two hymns, and the priest read something from a bible. We were all done in twenty minutes. We came back in a cab. When we parted, Dromond said he was very sorry for our loss.

Passing Ships by Rosie Cullen

Sharon pulled into the small car park that backed the headland. Butch and Sundance were already sniffing at the salt in the air and yapping to be released. Parked right up to the driftwood fence Sharon could spy the long empty stretch of beach. The sea too presented a lonely face. On the far horizon she could make out a tanker travelling up the coast but none of the white sailed dinghies or the roaring powerboats which populated the summer months. It was an indifferent sea, a mirror to the density of cloud above, slate gray and choppy, no gusting waves to attract the hardier windsurfers. At this time of the year few ventured down here at this fading time of day.

Sitting in the driver's seat, Sharon felt all at once overwhelmed with inertia. What was the point of it all? What was the point of any of it? A year now since Paul had reluctantly packed his bags. His presence still lingering in the detritus which he had left behind and which she felt incapable of clearing. Drawers filled with old reports and handbooks, homemade discs, his navy anorak with the torn pocket hanging in the utility room, a pair of worn flip flops. Small signposts, reminding her that the sprawling bungalow had once been invested with their shared dreams of a home together.

She felt guilty, she supposed, for asking him to leave, although she knew in her heart that the break had been long overdue; for ten years, a slow and painful withering of feeling and connection which they had both avoided looking square in the eye.

Sharon had known it would be up to her to make the final move. To be hard and ruthless, the villain of the piece, and everything that was against her nature. But Paul's slide into suffocating despair had stiffened her resolve. It was a matter of survival. Her last chance to escape the black hole of his yawning need, a void no one could surely fill, try as she had for over twenty years.

Here she was at forty-nine as washed up as the strings of seaweed fringing the tide line, two aging terriers for company, on a far-flung Antipodean shore. The bright lights of her youthful adventure dimming fast. No real friends other than of the casual variety, Australians were good at that—but none of substance. Paul had always been there, the centre of her life; whilst the chance for cultivating deeper friendships passed her by. So now she was alone and felt alone. The dogs whined, eager to feel the sand beneath their paws, the spray twitching at their nostrils.

"Okay. Okay," she assured and heaved herself out of the car.

***

Sharon loved this stretch of the New South Wales coastline; it really was the most beautiful place she could imagine and strolling along the length of the beach one of her constant pleasures. She hugged herself in to the onshore breeze and delighted in the way the dogs scampered up to the incoming waves and then rushed back as they broke, the froth fingering out to catch their short stubby legs. All at once they were joined by a black Labrador, young and playful. Sharon grinned, Sunny would see him off; Butch was the only dog Sundance ever let get a sniff of her. But Sharon took pity on the startled pup who was flopping from side to side as this ageing bitch snapped at his heels.

"Sunny!" she yelled. "Sunny, lay off the poor fellow, old girl!"

Sunny did no such thing of course; she was always of her own mind, unlike Butch who was wagging in a friendly way at the Labrador.

A sharp whistle came from the grassy bank above and the Labrador paused, turned about and then hurled himself towards his owner. The man came into view and dropped down on to the beach. He waved.

"He needs an old girl like that to teach him some manners." An open smiling face framed by a thick head of grey curls. "Was that a Yorkshire accent I heard?"

"Yes, Leeds."

"Hail fellow well met!" The man grinned and pointed to himself. "Scarborough."

"A long way from home."

"Maybe it was the sea air—I've always been a traveller."

"Passing through?"

"In a manner, live inland, twenty miles back, wife's an Aussie—but I'm away a lot, with the UN, all around South-East Asia." He added. "And you?"

She told him, the this and the that of her life, the simple mundane facts, a demanding but rewarding job working with refugees from Afghanistan, Myanmar. Ten minutes later and she realised that they were strolling along in a companionable way. Butch encouraged into play by the young dog Rover whilst Sundance maintained an aloof and dignified distance. Tony was five years older than herself but he had been a postgraduate student in Leeds when she was at the university and knew it well. Had, indeed, lived not far from her family home in Kirkstall. Had frequented some of the same bars and clubs where she had been that rude and drunken young goth with the dyed black spiky hair. They had probably passed each other.

The edge. That's what they both missed they confided. And sighed with the pleasure of remembering. The edginess of cities like Leeds and Liverpool and Manchester. Especially in those days. They laughed to remember the biting winter winds sweeping down The Headrow in Leeds, the battle to turn a corner into the full force of them.

Still, they were surrounded by all this natural wonder, the beach, the national park home to koala and wallaby, the crystal-clear river and lagoon, the most beautiful place in all his travels, Tony asserted. And the climate, that was a bonus. And then she was telling him about her 'round the world' ticket and how she had never made it beyond Sydney because she had met Paul and it had been sudden and overwhelming. She could see that Tony understood.

Kaia was his third wife, he confessed, much younger. They had a two-year old daughter, who kept him on his toes. A joy. Although he sometimes welcomed the missions to Laos or Cambodia just for the chance to sleep through the night, he admitted sheepishly.

They had traversed the length of the beach and were now on the return. The gloom of evening descending. What had it been? An hour? Two hours? Butch was lagging behind, tongue lolling, worn out by Rover's tireless energy. They drew close at last to the grassy bank.

Tony came to a halt and glanced at his watch. "My wife makes a great Thai Red Curry; you must come over some evening."

Sharon nodded but neither of them had pen or paper to jot down phone numbers. The invitation seemed enough anyway. They would hopefully meet again. And then he was gone, Rover racing on ahead. She watched the empty space, momentarily bereft of his presence; but then realised that Tony had left her something. That feeling of being herself again, of being alive in the moment.

***

Sharon opened the boot of her car and the dogs leapt in well satisfied with the unusual length of their evening run. She gazed down at the empty beach and out across the widening sea. The clouds were scattering and there was a glow to the day's end that hadn't been in it before.

The Weathermen—A Love Letter
by Aneeta Sundararaj

Anjali
Kuala Lumpur, Malaysia
24 October 2020
(Start of Scorpio Season)

Dear Roshan,

Last night, my mother wanted to know about the progress of the revised *jadagam* report from the astrologer after we gave Mr. Moorthy your wrong time of birth. To paraphrase Shakespeare, if what I told Mummy were played upon a stage now, I could condemn it as impossible fiction. It would have been criminal not to share what I said to her. I promise you that this is a light-hearted read compared to the prolonged uncertainty as we muddle through COVID-19 and the possibility of Emergency being declared in Malaysia.

You see, Daddy was a man of few words. However, what he did say was often so meaningful that it remained for life. Like when he referred to astrologers, numerologists and palmists collectively as, 'The Weathermen'.

"Those *jadagam* things they create," Daddy decided, "are as accurate as a weather report. When they say eight out of twelve 'houses' are good between a couple, look at the four that aren't."

My mother grumbled at his pessimism, but I learnt from this. The fact of the matter is that I couldn't care less what these reports say. I usually agree to get them done to please others and follow procedure. It's like preparing for my court cases.

Any lawyer worth her salt will tell you that although the paperwork is properly done, she must always be aware of being ambushed during the proceedings. I equate those four 'houses' that won't work in any union as an ambush in court. Will a marriage work in spite of these non-matching houses? That's the question, Roshan. More importantly, will ours?

Mr. Moorthy is probably sulking that we were careless with your time of birth. On the eve of the *atma shanti* prayers for the repose of Daddy's soul two years ago, he insisted that I, at the very least, buy some flowers. I'd asked him to bring absolutely everything as I had no clue where to get things like long-lasting camphor, betel leaves, turmeric paste and pure ghee. I rushed to the only florist whose roadside stall was still open at 7.30 p.m. When I told him what the flowers were for, he practically snatched a few wilting stalks out of my hand and marched to a cooler inside the shop lot.

"Moorthy Sir, ah?" he asked when he returned and began rolling a large bunch of fresh purple and yellow daisies in old newspapers. Adding a few stalks of rosebuds to the bunch for free, he said, "Take this. All new one."

I smiled. All of Alor Setar was petrified of this cantankerous priest whose reputation for not tolerating mistakes preceded him.

How to push him, Roshan, for our revised *jadagam* report? He'll scold me.

That's why I asked Krishnan for help. He's so funny. He makes me keep it a big secret that he's a devout Catholic. He's aware that I will tease him because it's the Bible-toting ones who will swear that they don't believe in all these *jadagam-badagam* things, but will also be the first to want their horoscopes read.

Still, I'm on the verge of giving up on Krishnan's 'astrologer contact' in Kerala. After six weeks, Smokey (as I've decided to call this astrologer) is probably still roaming the countryside looking for the ideal palm leaf, smoking it so that it's smooth, sharpening his quill and preparing the ink. Every time I ask Krishnan what's happening, his Whatsapp message is two words—*please wait*.

Finally, I turned to the 'the Wizard'. A pukka Tamil, imagine a seventy-eight-year-old man with sparse white hair that is styled with Brylcreem gel. He wears starched cotton shirts like the civil servants of the British Raj used to wear. From elbow down, though, he's a 1970s hippie espousing flower power. He wears at least three bracelets on either wrist made of various beads. On the right, he has amethyst to activate his crown chakra and rose quartz to harmonise the energies in his heart chakra. On the left, there's topaz to … I forget for which chakra. In his house, he converted the space where the skylight used to be into a windowless bedroom to align with the energies of *vaashtu* geomancy. That's the Wizard for you.

I gave him our details, but didn't dare tell him that this was all upside down. This *jadagam* thing should've been done before we met. That's the norm, no? First the report, then the parents meet, then the couple meets, then marriage. Like a proper Tamil drama.

How to tell the Wizard that we've known each other for two years already? He asked me which hospital you were working in. I told him that you've been in Mauritius for six months because of the pandemic then changed the subject.

The first astrologer the Wizard suggested was Master Yuvaraj from India. With COVID-19, Master's gone high-tech. At RM250.00, Master will present his report via

Zoom and I am allowed to ask as many questions as I like.

I opted for a local and cheaper weatherman. However, he's going to take time because I sent our details to the Wizard on a Tuesday. The astrologer can only accept Whatsapp messages on a Friday. That was yesterday. In the literary footsteps of Robinson Crusoe, I've chosen to name this one 'Friday'.

Incidentally, I can't understand why so many people are upset about the wrong time of birth issue. Like your mum telling me to take things easy. With all my insecurities, I wonder if she's annoyed with me. The thing is, I feel for her. Poor thing. I can barely remember details about my dachshund Gulabi (closest I had to a child) and your Mum has six children. Her giving me the wrong time of birth was bound to happen. If she knows the ridiculousness I've been through, she'll see that this is really nothing and very funny.

For example, there was Notchy (I don't bother remembering the names of previous suitors and I freely admit that I sometimes get them mixed up). His father was adamant that we meet only if our stars were aligned. Since we had 10 houses that matched, it was permissible for 'the boy' to call me. He spent a quarter of an hour describing his Amma's finger-licking *vengayam columbu*. Also, his darling niece was so clever because she could blow soapy bubbles when she was all of one. His only question was if I was willing to cook the same onion curry as his Amma.

Later in the day, he texted to inform (his word, not mine) me that we should 'take it up a notch'. I asked what this meant. He wanted me to go with him to Kluang to attend the wedding of the son of the lady who'd introduced us. That's like 250km from KL.

I responded with a 'let me think about it'. I've learnt never to reply with a firm no. Or even in the affirmative, for that matter. Always be non-committal as whatever 'the girl' says, however intelligent or honest, will inevitably be wrong and backfire.

Next, I put on my Spidey sensors, sent out feelers and made enquiries.

As it happens, Notchy was a little naughty.

Notchy had a twenty-year-old daughter from a previous shot-gun marriage. It was a *thali*-tying temple wedding which was never registered, thus rendering this child illegitimate. Now that he was fifty, he wanted legitimate children and his Amma was desperate for him to settle down. Notchy saw my photo and figured that I was worthy enough to be his baby-making machine. More so since two matching 'houses' were intimacy and family.

The other was Borty, some management-level person at AIG Insurance. Our charts matched in nine houses. Since I'm in my forties, he wanted me to buy medical insurance that covered fertility issues. He was worried that our children wouldn't be perfect and I must be willing to terminate an imperfect pregnancy. I am opposed to aborting a foetus for such trivial reasons. That didn't go down well.

Honestly, which child is perfect?

This also was mild compared with a prayer many years ago at the Nageswari temple in Bangsar. Imagine me, who suffers from ophidiophobia, shaking from head to toe, presenting a six-inch-tall cobra made of silver to the goddess whose name roughly translates to champion of snakes. Apparently, I had the curse of a snake in my subtle being—*naag dosham*—and that's why my sharp tongue repelled men. By making this gift to the goddess, the snake and I were free to find mates. How can I explain to people that since this invisible reptile's departure, my words are probably even more cutting now?

In all this, I still don't know what that word *jadagam* means. I thought it meant a report that sets out the suitability of a romantic match between two suitors. Now the Wizard has used a new one—*porutham.* My feeling is that no one genuinely knows what these words mean and I'm probably the first inquisitive one to ask.

What now, Roshan?

When I met the Wizard for tea, he echoed Mr. Moorthy's first supposedly inaccurate report and said that we must not delay. You and I are both no longer young. Nevertheless, there are chances that we'll become closer in 2021. The full moon is coming and, apparently, it's special because it's the first time this whole year that there's a full moon twice in one month. While sipping his piping hot *teh tarik,* the Wizard declared, "The time is right."

But right for what, Roshan?

And what does 'must not delay' mean?

I was desperate to seek clarification, but didn't dare.

Can you imagine what would have happened if I'd said, "Yes, we will not delay. Roshan and I will get married and procreate NOW!"

Naturally, my imagination ran wild. Although there's currently a whole ocean between us, you will marry me and somehow impregnate me this very night—an immaculate conception, at best. Still, Roshan, in nine months, we could have our own Christ-like child who will be highly intelligent with a lovely smile.

What are we to do when our weathermen—Mr. Moorthy, Smokey and Friday—eventually send their reports? Naturally, I expect to receive them in the aftermath of my fourth of November birthday because that's when Mars goes direct and communication is back to running smoothly.

What if we're not at all a match? What happens if one weatherman says we're a good match and other two say we're not? Do we choose the best of three? Do we never see each other again? Or, do we do Tamil drama style and elope? Must we sacrifice ourselves for love à la Shakespearean tragedy?

What do you think?

Muddles, cuddles and bubbles, my darling.

All my love, Anjali.

The Shadow Waved Back by Leena Batchelor

Inspired by a visit to Tintagel 2019, and all true.

Standing high on the cliffs overlooking Tintagel and the sea stands a country church, and amongst its wind-swept shadows, the ruined footprint of an older, Celtic church, lying hidden. St. Materiana, built between 1080 and 1150, is named after Madryn, a princess of Gwent, who evangelised the area around 500CE to exorcise the ancient rites of the Celts.

Colourful histories and the dark shades of death abound amongst the artefacts within; it is little wonder that these tales hang onto visitors' footsteps, those who are hardy enough to travail up the footpath and exposed hill to the small, stony objective on the horizon. The font is Norman, acquired from St. Julietta's chapel in Tintagel Castle; the rood screen dates from 1500 whilst the Bishop's Chair is late Tudor; the stone bench along the west and south walls is medieval. The south transept contains a Roman milestone bearing the name of the Roman emperor Caius Licinius, a rival to the Emperor Constantine (both bringers of the Christian faith to Rome) who put Licinius to death, proclaiming him to be Pagan. A lifebelt from the barque *Iota* commemorates the death of a cabin boy in 1893 in a shipwreck in nearby Bossiney Cove. I have no doubt that the stained-glass windows, in all their lead-speckled rainbow glory, created their own mosaic of life and stories past. Ghosts surely walked the paths between lichen-speckled graves salted by the unholy storms whistled up on many a winter's night.

My visit was led by an innate desire to find a peace from the noise of daily life; it's a cliché to say 'find myself', but I had felt a lack of direction during the spring, and the yearning pull to go to Tintagel, alone, could no longer be denied. Why Tintagel? Apart from my inherent love of history and anything Arthurian, I could think of no logical reason, but knew I had to answer the subliminal call or forever feel a sense of loss.

I found Tintagel to be unnerving at sunset. By day, I had wandered (and wondered at) the village, yet at twilight the sense pervaded of a place having gone to sleep, in pause before the magic of sunset. On one such evening, my eyes were drawn to the apparition of a light upon the hill, brooding over the tides awaiting the pull and cooling colour of summer moonlight. Was this a beacon, or a flicker of a past calling to those lost on the seas or in the coolness of Merlin's Cave below? An image filled my mind of the church and its lights being lighthouse keepers for souls and ships alike, both calling and warning, across moss-waved moor and rocky shore. I wondered whether there was a lonely rector still sermonising to wraith-filled pews, cobwebs filling the gaps between the hymns and psalms? A chill whispered across the waves, suffusing the mists, singing older songs and rituals; spells to call to life the Tuath Dé of the Celtic Otherworld, to open the gates to Avalon. Suddenly, the juxtaposition of old magic and religion was lost; they now co-existed in a meld of time and space that pervaded reality, drew aside gossamer veils.

I recalled how the bells had rung unheard on the Sabbath day. Had the lichen silenced the bells calling the faithful to their rest, allowing forgotten souls to float through the streets of shadows after sunset?

Deep in thought, my feet traced their own path to a seat overlooking Merlin's Cave, St. Materiana's shadowing the encroaching nightfall; the resonance of past life reverberating in the air across the water. Near enough now to see the darkness of the church windows as the candle snuffed out, I convinced myself the faint light had been merely a reflection of some passing car, un-remarkedly continuing on its journey. My conviction was short-lived when the silhouette walked to, and paused at, the window, the shine of her eyes (for I could feel her sex as clearly as my own) illuminating the awakening path to my soul.

The image of the shade imprinted upon my mind as if on the silver of a photograph, in the way the silver of a mirror greyed with age would look back at you, a forgotten moment captured forever in the camera of my mind. Compelled by a warning throbbing deep in my nerves, I raised a hand in greeting as somehow I recognised that to ignore this revenant would bring dire consequence to bear.

Darkened in time and thought and intent was the shadow that waved back to me. I discerned in that moment my innermost desires would become mine, if I but dared call to ancient rites.

No shadow crosses my path now but I acknowledge the accosting of my light, and wave it on its return to the dark.

Passing On by Polly Palmer

Sam sat on the step easing his aching limbs. Behind him his mother clattered pans and called the younger children to their tea. It had been a baking day today so they would have a pie, left over from those she sold to passing travellers. He heard his father come in from the orchard with apples and vegetables for tomorrow.

A familiar delectable smell wafted in from the kitchen. His mother swiftly dealt out portions of pie and the little ones fell upon the food. His father looked tired; he ate slowly and didn't finish. They chatted about mill business: the flooding, the crop spoiling in the fields, the profit after the owner's cut.

"Time for you to step up lad," said his father. Sam stared at him in dismay, rebuking himself for failing to see the slowing of pace, difficulty on the mill stairs, laboured breathing. He felt sorrow and exhilaration in equal measure, followed by consuming guilt.

He set off to the mill for the night shift. The wind was rising, gusting across the fields. The last fiery rays of the setting sun struck the mill roof; the alders whipped and flexed in the approaching storm. He heard thunder, deep and ominous, and fretted over the winter wheat.

On the corner of the lane, he almost collided with a girl. Their eyes met and she held his gaze.

"I'm looking for Mrs. Hacker. She's looking for a girl to help—cooking and keeping chickens and that."

As he directed her, Sam flushed scarlet.

"Maybe I'll see you!" she called over her shoulder, laughing.

***

Sam remembered that first meeting all summer long. One evening in July he was sitting on the step when she slipped past and sat down beside him. He struggled for something to say to keep her there. She looked sideways at him, waiting.

"Hello, Eliza. How do you like working with my mother then?" He felt elated to have formed a sentence.

"I like it, she's taught me loads." He felt her eyes piercing the back of his skull. "It could be a proper little business, you know."

"How?"

"You could open a shop and make bread and cakes as well as pies. I'm good at baking."

Sam frowned. "Where though? The mill's rough, and too far out of the village." He groaned inwardly at his negative tone.

"Why don't you and your dad build here? A shop at the front and the kitchen behind? A cellar too for extra bread ovens? And an upstairs to store the flour and maybe …" She stopped and put her hand over her mouth, her eyes widening with embarrassment.

"What? Maybe what?" Her excitement was infectious.

"Well, for them's as run it to live in!" She turned that fearless stare on him. "You and me!"

***

As summer turned to autumn, Sam and his father

began building a lean-to shelter against the cottage wall. They put an old range in the back and during the winter Eliza made and sold baked goods alongside his mother. They would huddle round the stove for a while before he walked her home, racing past the darkened mill as children did, hooting and screeching as the mist rose over the pond.

As the days began to lengthen again Eliza began to stay over in the ancient cottage. Secretly she crept from the little ones' bedroom at night to find Sam in the warm bakery. On May Day they were gone until darkness fell, returning flushed with cider and brushing off grass and blossom.

"You tucking into them pasties, Eliza? You'm looking quite round and rosy these days." The girl blushed and looked at Sam, and his mother smiled to herself.

People began to come from the next village to buy bread and pies. The estate manager came to inspect and was impressed, relishing new income. The vicar dropped by one evening at closing time, curious to see the young couple folk were talking about.

"This is a fine setup," he said, taking in the neat little shop. "Did you do all this yourselves?"

"With my dad—he supervised. I'm not so good at measuring. I just do the donkey work."

"It was hard digging out the cellar," added Eliza.

"Did you do that then, young lady?" the vicar said, smiling broadly. She smirked and shook her head. He understood and changed the subject.

"If you want to learn to do the books, my wife teaches a group your age just starting out in trade. I'll get her to drop by."

When he had gone, Eliza ran to hug Sam. He resisted, pursing his lips.

"What's wrong? That'd be wonderful!"

He sighed. "I can't see to read Eliza. You do it. I don't need book learning to do what I do."

She stood open-mouthed for a moment. "Why did you never tell me?" she said, half in anger. "It's a new world now! There are invoices and orders!"

She put her arms around him, burying her face in his chest. "Leave it with me," she said. "I've had an idea".

***

Sam sat at the bench where he always supervised the milling of the grain. The hot afternoon sun caught motes of dust settling silently on wood and metal, a soft velvet shroud. There was a time when there was so much flour it would choke him. When they were young Eliza used to worry about his worsening cough; he smiled as he remembered her telling him off for the long hours he worked.

"You're just working to put money in their pockets," she would complain, hands on hips. "They've got mills all up this river and they pay you a pittance."

He remembered with pleasure how Eliza would come down to the mill as their children grew, always bringing a treat straight from the oven. They felt part of the new age; railways, steam, mass manufacturing, entrepreneurship. She loved the quaking rumble of the millstones and the roaring mill race, shouting above the din and singing from the top of the building as the flour bags filled. Sam taught her how to sample the grist and fine tune the stones. When at last she struggled with the stairs, breathless and wheezing, she would set the wheel going and race to the top floor to inspect the milled flour.

He remembered his father and his loss of power at the same age. Eliza still had all her youthful energy; she took to wearing dungarees, tying her long curls back and rolling up her sleeves. Together they had built on his parents' legacy; making a home, building a bakery, learning new skills, running a business. As the new century rolled on, he watched her with pride as she made flour and bread for the war effort.

Sam sighed, looking out over the sunken boats in the mill pond to the crumbling lockkeeper's cottage. Little by little the railways had taken over; the flour barges no longer stopped at the lock; the canal silted up. As trade dwindled the owner had lost interest. Now Sam worked on alone, grinding flour for the bakery, keeping the old mill going.

Eliza called to him from the top floor. She ran down, waving a document, to where he sat musing at the window. "Sam! Look what I found! They're closing the mill! When d'you think they'd have told us?" Sam squinted at the paper, then reached into his pocket for his magnifying glass. He remembered suddenly Eliza pressing it into his hand all those years ago. "There! It was my grandma's. Now you can see to learn your words and numbers!"

He read the sale inventory of the machinery and the valuation of the mill and farm.

All these decades, working the clock round while they made money off my hard graft. None of this is mine.

He took her hand. She was flushed with righteous fury and he frowned at the paper to hide the sudden tears in his eyes.

"Well Eliza, no surprise there. We mustn't mind, we'll

manage. You finish this batch and we'll load the cart."

He struggled to control his despair, hearing her crashing around below, venting her rage on the sack barrow. When she had left with the last bags he swept up. Eliza was furious, demanding to see the owner, the agent, the squire. For once, though, he was not persuaded by her fighting spirit.

He climbed to the next floor, pulling himself up each step. He shook out the broom and pan there and stamped on the loose boards. Thick white clouds of flour rose into the air, filtering the sunlight. Coughing, he piled some paper bags on the sunny bench with the sale catalogue, crumpling its pages into balls.

Then he propped the magnifying glass against the paper pyramid, focusing precisely the rays of the setting sun.

Evensong by John Hargreaves

Two memories from the period just before my wedding—forty years ago—popped into my mind as the train pulled out of Crewe on its way to Birmingham New Street: my having to remind Martin repeatedly that I wanted to walk down the aisle a virgin, and playing Tea for the Tillerman obsessively on his record player. The emotional intensity in Cat Stevens' voice promised my young self the earth. Then came Morning has Broken and I knew it had to be our opening hymn.

Rattling towards Stafford in the tin box of a train, I could hear my mother's shrill objection. "That's for a christening! Why put notions in people's heads?"

Praise for the singing, praise for the morning

Praise for them springing fresh from the world

Blackbird had spoken like the first bird and Martin would never guess the extent to which that voice aroused me. But he enjoyed the sex.

As did I. Every day after we were married. Sometimes twice. I always liked the morning ones the best.

I used to like these trains with noisy engines that vibrate under your seat. Cold in winter and hot in summer, they feel more like buses stopping for ordinary people heading to the shops, coming home from school, meeting up with friends.

On the line to Hereford I've seen people put their arms out to tell the driver they want to get on. From Birmingham out to Lichfield City, a dozen stops in as many miles.

There used to be a bustle about these trains that I could get lost in, jammed up against all sorts, mostly polite, listening-in: who's picking up Liam from Scouts, what's for tea. Nowadays there's more space than people but some still acknowledge me with shining eyes above their masks as they head for their isolated seats. I choose one of them now to watch as I imagine sharing my memories aloud.

Our sex life remained spirited, I tell him, though we made love just three or four times a week after Susan was born. And just two or three times after Stephen. With a hiatus for a few weeks around each birth. No idea how Martin coped with that. As the children grew we had to timetable our lovemaking but our passion proved schedule-proof. Martin liked me calling him a tiger in the bedroom. Sometimes he called me a vixen.

I take proper trains, the kind with locomotives up front, when I venture further afield: Carlisle, Bristol, Ely. I like to take a seat in the quiet coach and mix my daydreaming with a light novel. Alongside singletons mostly. People with suitcases. Mature businessmen working on laptops.

Martin was a businessman before he retired. Twenty-nine when we married, against my twenty-one. My mother warned me.

I feel more relaxed in those proper trains, and more daring. I pick a man – sometimes two if I'm feeling wild -- and I recall some of my more adventurous exploits in the bedroom. Mine and Martin's I should say; always a pair. Anglo-Saxon words in my silent recollections and explicit visuals. We were ever bold. *Praise for them springing.* Confidence leads to exploration and adventure feeds confidence. A virtuous circle.

My mother, who could never imagine sex over fifty, was okay with a nine-year difference in older couples, but not when we were in our twenties. "You've no idea where he's been," she said.

Now I'm in my sixties and I've taken care of my body. I enjoy looking good. When the man facing me two booths along lowers his paper for a male gaze, I project ardour and *dare* him to think of me as 'well preserved'.

Whereas Martin is well past seventy now and the years between us make a world of difference. Exercising his libido has not served to keep it in shape. Nor do the little blue pills help any more.

I wonder if the man behind the newspaper has me down as a woman with unmet needs.

Martin worries more about how he is letting me down than he does about his high blood pressure. First he blamed it on his retirement and his loss of stature as an executive managing a large staff. Then he blamed his inflexible sleep pattern: early to bed and early to rise. I like to read with the light on and sleep in. His prostate gets him up two or three times a night and however subtly he sneaked out to pee, he knew it woke me. Finally he blamed his snoring. When he learned my earplugs didn't help, he banished himself to the spare room.

I can tell I'm losing the man opposite and two seats along who's almost my age. Prostrates and ear plugs all over my face. I smile at him disarmingly. When the train stops, the man leaves his paper on the seat next to him and gets off. I feel deflated.

My favourite day trips are Chester-- almost on my doorstep-- Lichfield, Liverpool, and best of all Birmingham. To the men whose paths I cross on these adventures it must seem an unlikely hobby for me to take up, especially when I tell them that I'm not religious or notably musical or into architecture.

It was Martin who suggested the idea. "A different

cathedral every Wednesday afternoon," he said. "Choral evensong broadcast by the BBC. You can hear them live, and I'll listen to them on the Radio."

Not the Lionesses playing football. Not a play at every West End theatre. Radio Three's Outside Broadcasting Team, for goodness sake. And choirboys in cassocks.

But when Martin rattled off the names of the cathedral cities in the BBC's schedule, I warmed to the idea. And there was a familiar quality to his enthusiasm. I couldn't get out of my head the notion that what Martin was suggesting had sex at the core of it.

"Just because I'm a boring stay-at-home doesn't mean that you should be too." Looking out for me in our new circumstance, for which he felt responsible.

"You should be having fun. You can have fun for the pair of us."

I became convinced that he was edging me into a new arena.

"Who would have thought evensong my thing?" I said.

"You'll enjoy the travel. You've always liked trains. You'll get chatting. You'll make friends among the other groupies."

I had to be there half an hour early but that was fine because I could take an early train and have lunch and do a little window shopping. I didn't like coming home late at night and if the BBC was in Canterbury, say, or Truro, it wasn't easy to make the last train anyway. Then I found my own choral evensongs. Always on a Wednesday. I liked the routine. It soon came to feel like ritual. When I got home Martin would have dinner ready for me, with candles and wine, and have me recount my adventures.

"There was a rather dashing-looking man in the seat

opposite," I said one night when I got back from Blackburn. Martin wanted to know all about him. What we talked about. What made me think him handsome. At bedtime – Martin's bedtime – I said I was tired and would fall straight asleep so why didn't he join me? And he did. We kissed and cuddled and it felt lovely, though he decamped in the middle of the night.

I animated Martin's Wednesday evenings with accounts of my little flirtations: the fashion designer who loved leather and waxed lyrical about my gloves and handbag, the six-footer in the crowded carriage who apologised for having no room for his legs and smiled cheekily when we came to a touching accommodation. The more I stretched these encounters in the re-telling, the more eager Martin was to accept my invitation for an early night together.

It was Martin's idea that I follow the BBC to more remote destinations and stay overnight in a hotel. I enjoyed the proper trains, whose relative comfort encouraged daydreaming and whose social mix stimulated my imagination. Martin said I should be sure to take my phone and he would call me after dinner for an account of my exploits.

After a few of these overnight trips Martin told me he was thrilled by my spirited independence and I took it as a cue to turn off my phone the moment I left home. The next morning I'd linger at my hotel, have a leisurely lunch, and arrive home in the early evening. Martin would be on tenterhooks. Candlelit dinner waiting. Bubbly on ice. Over dessert I would talk freely and fancifully. Sometimes we would stay together all night.

Once, coming back from Norfolk, I missed a connection and didn't get home until eleven. Martin was distraught. I wondered if he thought I might not come home at all.

After that he insisted we both keep our phones on for messaging. He said we should have a 'safe' word that could be sent quickly – 'red' would be the obvious choice. We'd never gone as far as that in our younger sex play and though it didn't make a lot of sense, I could tell that he found the idea exciting. He said I could use the other traffic lights when appropriate.

I tapped in 'green' as my rattletrap pulled into New Street. Then, recalling the visual detail of my erotic recollections for the benefit of the man behind the newspaper, I changed it to 'amber'. Martin could make of that what he liked.

In my rush to see my man I considered taking a taxi but the afternoon sun was glorious and it was only a six minute walk so I opted for delayed gratification. At the top of Temple Street I turned left on Temple Row. I could see that the west door of the cathedral was open and I flushed with anticipation.

I took my usual seat at the back of the nave and composed myself. Though there were many empty seats, someone shuffled along the pew and sat right next to me. I didn't want distractions but no sooner had I glanced up than he said, "Hello, I've seen you at choral evensong before. Various places. I thought I should introduce myself." He held out his hand. "I'm Jonathan."

I shook it feebly. He looked like he was dressed for the opera.

"I've remarked to myself how well you dress," he said, and then added quickly: "I don't mean to sound forward. I think this music, this experience of the music, demands respect and dress is an obvious way of giving it. I'm sure you agree."

"I'm not here for the music." After an afternoon of talking to strangers silently, I spoke my thoughts out loud: "I sometimes wish they'd sing a song I could relate to. Like Morning Has Broken."

Sacrilege. Distress on his face. He said, "I understand it's popular at funerals. Among those blissfully untroubled by The Day of Reckoning, I presume."

And that, I realised, was what transfixed me in the stained-glass window over my shoulder. It was The Day of Judgement and even as we sat there waiting for the Outside Broadcasting Team to finish their sound checks, it cast rays of brilliant colour over the floor beside me. There was my one true man. His body, draped in the folds of an exquisite red robe, turned and rose on the ball of a naked foot to connect in powerful symmetry with the Archangel Michael above. Though facing away, it was clearly Martin. Comfortable and ready in his gorgeous body. The scene was disconcertingly lush. I was so turned on by the prospect of communing with it as soon as the service was over, I stepped into the aisle and took out my phone to text another 'amber'.

But there was a message waiting for me. It would prove to be my last ever from Martin.

It said simply, 'red.'

A Contained Life by Rebecca Kinnarney

Debra decants what's left of the cherry tomatoes into the small round plastic bowl and eases on the blue lid. Not strictly Tupperware, this one, but no-one calls their Tupperware cupboard 'the plastic container cupboard'. She stands and stares out of the tiny kitchen window at the house opposite. *It's like Hoovers*, she thinks. *Barely anyone has an actual Hoover anymore but no-one says that they are going to Dyson the living room.*

'*Other vacuum cleaner brands are available.*' She hears a BBC voice in her head.

She opens the large American style fridge and, for a second, admires the array of 'Tupperware' boxes inside, neatly stacked, filled with all manner of leftovers. Debra is a woman of order; a place for everything and everything in its place. God, her mother had been full of clichés but some of them had stuck. If Debra was honest with herself, a lot of them had stuck. She slams the fridge door to, a little more firmly than she should. Gently, she opens it again, checking the seal. She's waited a very long time for a fridge like this; one of those upright ones with the freezer next to it. Like a stainless-steel cupboard. Or coffin.

The pips on the radio interrupt Debra's thoughts. She seals up the Tupperware tomb. *Must press on.* She picks up the rectangular plastic lunchbox and drops it into her canvas book bag. She needs to be out of the house by 8:04 to get to work on time. She could leave later but she likes to get off the Tube at Bayswater and walk down through the park to work.

The morning constitutional sets her up well for the day, although, she's noticed of late that the walk has been taking fractionally longer.

She might need to start leaving home earlier. Right now, though, she can't countenance any change to her routine, so she'll just have to pick up her pace a little.

***

At lunchtime, the park is surprisingly empty. Debra and Eve have no problem finding a bench to sit on in the gentle September sun. This is not one of those September days which surprises you with the ferocity of its heat. This is one which whispers of woollen coats and of scarves shoved in bags, just in case the temperature drops later.

"Let me guess," says Eve. "It's Thursday, so it must be ham and grainy mustard with a few cherry tomatoes on the side. And the obligatory cereal bar."

Debra smiles in response.

"How many years have you been making those packed lunches, Deb?"

"Well, ever since Jim and I got married. So, twenty-seven years, four months, eighteen days. Give or take."

"Seems to me that there's been a lot of giving and not much taking from your side."

Debra's eyes shine with sadness.

"Sorry, sorry." Eve lays her hand on her friend's arm. "That was rubbish of me."

"It's ok." Debra knows that Eve, a good twenty years younger than Debra, could never understand the choices that she's made. Eve only sees them as sacrifices. Debra knows this for a fact. They've spoken about it often enough.

"Tell him to make his own bloody sandwiches," used

to be one of Eve's frequent refrains. But Debra has never wanted to tell Jim that. She's always wanted to do all of those little things for him. She wants to iron five shirts for him every Sunday night: five identical blue cotton shirts, five identical white handkerchiefs, five identical pairs of black socks. Routine like this doesn't suit everyone but it suits Debra.

When she met Jim, she'd been looking for an antidote to the chaos of her childhood. She'd been looking for stability, stolidity. Not that she'd known that, of course. You don't consciously know those things when you're twenty and just about to graduate. She just knew that she was always drawn to older, as she perceived it, wiser men. Not the flashy men looking for a trophy wife -- that, Debra was definitely not -- but the older men who knew who they were and didn't need to go off on adventures to find themselves.

"Deb? Deb?" Eve's voice brings Debra forward nearly thirty years. "What do you think about Sara and David then? What's going to happen?"

Eve is talking about the soap opera which they both love. Eve always knows how to get the conversation and the friendship back on track. Debra envies her social ability.

"Oh, I missed it again yesterday evening. Fill me in."

The rest of the lunchtime is spent in frivolous discussion about TV, work gossip and tales of Eve's erratic sister's exploits on the 'heading for thirty and desperate' dating circuit. Eve's words, not Debra's.

***

Dead on 5.30, Debra is out of the door. She speed-walks to the Tube station. No gentle walk home through the park. She hasn't time to waste at this end of the day.

On the Tube, she stands clutching the greasy handrail and feels the sweat running down the backs of her legs; September evenings on the Underground are like stepping into a sauna. The human heat builds through the day and reaches its steaming peak during rush hour. She gazes around the carriage at the shirts with their damp patches, at the hair plastered to heads. The only passengers who look fresh and clean are the people living an upside-down life. The nightshift workers at the sky-scraping hospital.

As they spew out onto the pavement, Debra gazes up at the great concrete monstrosity, looming over the small estate where she and Jim had bought their house two decades ago. They'd joked about how convenient it would be living in the shadow of the hospital. Debra had said it would be good for when they had children and she could just waddle round there, give birth and waddle home again. Jim had been silent. The waddle never happened.

Debra feels herself being propelled towards the road. A young man, suit jacket hooked on the index finger of one hand, ubiquitous mobile phone in the other, has pushed into her in his hurry to get to a drinks appointment or to pick up a ridiculously over-priced bottle of wine in the local ridiculously over-priced supermarket. He doesn't even see Debra. She's not offended. She's used to it. That's the way she likes it.

The push, though, spurs her to get a move on. At home, she performs a perfunctory freshen up and changes her blouse. Almost ready.

She opens the Tupperware cupboard and takes out a box shaped like an individual cake slice. She only found these a couple of weeks ago. They'd been on promotion at the supermarket when she'd gone to do the big shop. 'The box you never knew existed and now can't live without.'

They were right. She'd needed this years ago. Wrapping the daily slice of cake in tin foil had always been fraught with problems, especially if she'd put a generous coating of butter icing on the top. These boxes would have solved all sorts of problems. She bought two.

Now, she drops a slice of dense chocolate cake into the box and seals the lid carefully. This is Jim's favourite cake. She puts the enormous box containing the rest of the cake back into the fridge.

She leaves the house, clutching her canvas tote, and carefully locks the front door. She isn't going far or for very long but the days are gone when you could leave the door open and know that the neighbours would keep an eye out.

***

The ward is roasting when Debra gets there. They've cracked open the windows as much as they can but it isn't making the slightest difference. There's just no air here. Debra puts on her widest smile and greets the nurse on duty. "Evening, Samuel. How are you?"

"Very well, Mrs. Jackson. You?"

"Hot!"

They both chuckle. Social wheels oiled, Debra moves down the ward, forcing herself to keep up a brisk pace. Her legs feel like a cartoon cat's, wanting to run backwards.

Jim's bed is by the window. If he looks out, he's got a view of sky. If he doesn't, he's got ceiling. Today he's chosen ceiling.

"Evening, love," Debra says, patting his hand. Jim's eyes flicker at her. The muscles in his face twitch, lifting his mouth slightly.

"There's a lovely smile," she says. "Looks like you're having a good day." Debra pulls the high-backed chair closer to the bed, sits down and proceeds to recount the events of the day. They'd always done this, told each other about their day. Each day had been more or less the same as the next but it didn't stop them. She'd tell him about the people she'd seen on her walk through the park and how blue Crombie was back on the bench at lunchtime, this time with a different woman. He'd tell her how Janine in accounts had made another mistake with the Bradshaw file and how he'd had to phone Bradshaw's himself to smooth things over. She'd tell him how good he was at that kind of thing and how the firm were lucky to have him.

Jim, now, is silent but Debra still has a day to recount.

She knows that she mustn't stay long because he gets very tired. So, she wipes the corners of his mouth with the soft tissues she's brought with her, opens the bedside locker and takes out the plastic boxes inside. She puts them straight into her bag and brings out the cake-slice-shaped box.

"I've brought your favourite." Jim's eyes flicker again. "I'll pop it on the top here, so that it doesn't get forgotten."

She hesitates.

"Unless you'd like a little bit now?"

Jim closes his eyes.

Debra leans and kisses his forehead. "See you in the morning, love." Jim's breathing has changed and she knows he's already drifting into sleep. She knows every sound he makes and recognises what every breath indicates. Twenty-seven years listening to someone's breathing is a long time.

***

Back in their tiny kitchen, Debra opens the plastic boxes. All full of days-old food. She pulls back the lid of the cake-slice-shaped box which she's brought home with her. A blue furry mass inside. She feels the anger rising. Why couldn't the nurses at least just empty the food out? It's short-lived, though. She knows they're stretched beyond capacity. She also knows that they probably think she's, at best, deluded if she thinks he's going to be able to eat any of the things she brings in. She can't help herself though. Take the cake, for example. She's been baking a cake for him every week for twenty-seven years. You don't just stop doing something like that. She had to keep things as steady as she could and these routines were the things which steadied 'The good ship Debra', as Jim always called it.

Debra sets about cleaning all of the containers she's brought home with her. Her phone pings. *How are things?* It's Eve.

No change. Debra types back.

She receives a thumbs-up in response. Eve knows that, for Debra, no change is good.

The draining board is now stacked with plastic boxes and Debra goes into the hall to get her own empty lunch box from her book bag. The box isn't there. She's left it at work. She can picture it on the corner of her desk. She never leaves it at work. She never forgets things.

Debra crumples onto the bottom stair and begins to cry.

The Right Place by Sven Camrath

Tuesday

If he died here, nobody would find his corpse. The thought soothes him. Lichen-covered slabs surround him; their once-crisp inscriptions weathered away like the memories of those buried beneath. He breathes in the familiar smell of damp moss and rotten leaves, the calm embracing him like a shroud.

Behind thorny thickets, pricking anyone daring to intrude, is his hiding spot, far away from the living. The crumbling and overgrown crypt keeps him out of sight, hiding him from prying eyes. He is glad he hasn't encountered a single person crying over a cadaver in the ground this morning. Such a violent display of emotion is alien to him.

The rain-soaked soil squelches under his boots on his way to the fallen obelisk in the centre of his sacred place. Once, it must have been a centrepiece, the pride of a mason; it had toppled and broken into two big chunks. This is where he sits, listens, and waits day after day after day. He brushes off the wet leaves that had fallen on the jagged blocks during last night's storm. He sits on the cold, hard surface, his backpack between his legs. He takes out his weighty thermos, and with a low metallic clonk, puts it next to him. The crypt is behind him; watching him, hiding him, protecting him.

He produces a small, gray device from the pack. With the flick of a switch, its display lights up with a faint red glow. The needle stabs towards the far end of the meter, and once the surge of electricity disperses, it sinks back listlessly. The red light is the only indication that the device is not dead. It is capable of detecting faint electromagnetic fields, like the one from his neighbour's television, never ceasing its plastic drone through the thin sheets of suffocating drywall. Here, in a place that has never known electricity, the needle stubbornly refuses to move, day after day after day. But he is patient.

A second box appears in his hands, black and dull plastic covered with knobs and buttons, a chrome antenna protruding. The lettering on the plastic wore off long ago. A pair of well-worn headphones strangles the device. Their once bright, yellow foam is brittle and has taken on the color of dried pus, but they still work after all these years. He slowly unravels their cord and puts them on. He extends the antenna and turns one the knobs until he feels the familiar click. With closed eyes he drifts into communion with the device in his hands. The white noise of quickly changing frequencies fills his ears.

"What's that?"

Startled, he jolts from his bench and spins around. The cable snags on his jacket and pulls the headphones from his ears, throwing them onto the wet ground. Ahead of him stands a young woman; she would not be a day over twenty-five, not much younger than himself. She wears a puffy green jacket, black leggings, a matching beanie, and pale skin. She audibly chews a piece of gum. A melange of stale, cold cigarette smoke and mint invades his nose. She gives him a cheeky smile, a fresh scratch on her chin. How had she found him?

His heart is racing. He bends down to pick up the headphones. A large piece of foam had broken off. The woman pays no attention to him and instead peers at the motionless needle on the bench.

"Hey, I've seen one of these," she says, stepping closer towards the device. "That's one of these ghost detector thingies, right?"

That *thingie* was a finely calibrated EMF meter, but what did she know?

"You're hunting for ghosts, aren't you?" A glimmer of excitement in her eyes.

He hates it when amateurs call them ghosts; they are spirits.

He grabs the meter and slips it into his pocket to save it from her prying eyes.

"In a cemetery?" she stifles a laugh. "Of *all* the places, you are looking for ghosts in a *graveyard*? It's a cool place and all, but *come on*!"

Is she making fun of him? She's the one that has no idea about these things. He can feel his face getting hot. Her eyes wide open, she looks around his sanctuary like a child at a carnival.

"Man, I wish the others were here! This is going to be such an awesome hangout spot!"

The knot in his stomach tightens.

She moves her bony hands from her mouth back to one of the large marble chunks. For a split-second, he sees a piece of the woman's face stuck to the back of his bench; the chewing gum the same spent color as her skin. She pulls a packet from her jacket. She rips off the crinkling cellophane and lets it fall to the ground. She sticks a cigarette between her pale, thin lips, and gives him an expectant look. After he stands unmoving for an uncomfortable amount of time, she rolls her eyes and pats her pockets. She produces a plastic lighter and flicks it repeatedly. Each failed attempt is followed by a mumbled swear until she finally lights her cigarette. She takes a deep drag and closes her eyes.

"You gotta go to places with tormented souls," smoke trails her as she further desecrates his space. "The ones that still have unfinished business in this world and want revenge or something."

It's clear to him, she has no idea what she's talking about. He stifles a cough as the smoke reaches him. He longs for the calming smell of decay.

She leans against one of the moss-covered slabs, looking up into the bone-gray sky as she exhales another cancerous cloud. "Got a lot of free time on my hands, so I watch tons of ghost hunting shows. I mean, they're probably fake, but I did some *research*."

He doubts she even knows what that word means.

"Found all kinds of videos and photos on the web. Really creepy stuff you just can't explain, you know?" He barely hears her as the blood rushes through his ears.

"But yeah, *this* place?" she looks back at the crypt. "People don't die here; it's just where we bury them. You have to go to, like, an abandoned asylum or the scene of an unsolved murder. Places with —" she says, swirling her cigarette around in the air as if summoning a spell, "Energy, you know?"

He can feel a headache coming on; every word of hers becoming a painful stab.

She points at his hand. "Hey, is that *ghost radio*?"

At first, he doesn't understand. Then he realizes, she means the *spirit box*. He had been clutching it ever since she barged in, the headphones still hissing with static.

"Let me see it," she takes a step towards him, one hand reaching for his prized possession. He steps back and hastily stuffs the spirit box into his backpack. He grabs his thermos, metal ringing out as it scrapes against the marble. Now she is paying attention to him.

"I, uh – I have to get back to my friends," She drops her half-smoked cigarette, the wet soil suffocating it with a sizzle. "They are probably looking for me," is the last thing he remembers her saying.

Wednesday

No one mourns. An old man makes gravestone rubbings but doesn't notice him. His refuge is just as he had left it yesterday. At once the pressure sloughs off of him. He picks up the wet cigarette and the cellophane, wrinkling his nose as he puts them in a small trash bag. Yesterday his mind had not been in the right spot to clean up, he feels guilty for not taking better care of his space. He wipes his hands on his coat and walks over to the broken obelisk. A few more leaves have died and fallen. He gently wipes them off.

He sits down and pulls the thermos from his backpack, his brows furrowed as he feels the dented surface. Then he retrieves the EMF meter and flicks it on.

A smile appears on his lips as its needle jitters back and forth in the blood-red glow. He quickly pulls out the spirit box, puts on the headphones, and begins to listen. He takes a deep breath and catches a whiff of stale, cold cigarette smoke. Turns out she had been right about something after all.

Someone, No-one by Hilary Coyne

A door slams and I wake up. My head is on something soft and my feet are pressing against a hard surface. I open one eye; it feels crusty and my vision is blurred. I don't know where I am. My head throbs and my mouth is dry and sore. I lift my head slowly pushing strands of greasy blonde hair out of my face and look straight into the eyes of a Tyrannosaurus Rex. It is stuffed. A child's toy. Where the hell am I? I rub my eyes. Pain shoots across the bridge of my nose, and I feel a grittiness on my skin. I'm in a child's bedroom. In his bed. I look at the pillow and see dried blood and vomit where my head was a moment ago. There's no-one else here but I hear voices beyond the door. There is an anger in their tone that makes my stomach flip. I hear snatches of the conversation:

"Someone's been sitting…"

—a man's voice—

"…eaten my..."

A woman. And then: "eaten it all up!"

A child's plaintive wail.

Footsteps then. Fast, urgent, coming up the stairs and then reaching the door to the room, about to come in. Shit, I think. Remembering.

***

I saw him pretty much every night of the week outside the tube station. He always gave me whatever change he had and a bit of chat. He was friendly in that kind of posh, condescending way that people like him are. I worked with his sort in the temp jobs I had after I dropped out of uni –

back when I was still holding it all together. He probably calls the security guy *mate* and introduces his P.A. as *the real boss* in that jovial way of people who know they're at the top of the tree and are used to getting their own way.

He was a decent bloke though. He even remembered my name and asked if I was doing okay. Had enough to eat. I wasn't. Didn't. But I told him *yeah* and *no problem, but cheers all the same, God bless*. It's what you're supposed to say. You have about thirty seconds to massage their virtue and make them feel like they've done a *good thing* so they can go home to their warm homes and their families feeling pleased with themselves. That's for them. For me it's just common sense.

I want—need—another 50p tomorrow. I'd found this spot a few months ago and came here most nights from about 4 or 5 o'clock to catch the commuters arriving home. Lots of city types with plenty of cash. Although the really posh ones never give you anything. They couldn't even bear to look at you as if your obvious failure might be infectious. Most people were pretty generous though and Mr. Behr was one of the best.

A few times a month he would get in on a later train than usual and he'd give me a big grin, his mouth tinged red from wine, and most times also a tenner rather than just loose change. One of those nights I noticed after he'd walked away that he'd dropped his Oyster card. I picked it up and ran after him. I wasn't very fast because my knee was still a bit dodgy from the latest run-in with Kev. I loped along at a distance and caught up with him just before one of the streets with all the trees and the big houses, Woodland Way. He called me an absolute star and gave me twenty quid, said if I ever needed anything just to let him know. Then he was off, walking briskly up the road.

I should have gone back then to my spot. The station

would still be busy for ages yet. I was curious though and I followed him. I saw where he went in through a painted gate surrounded by a thick hedge. He stood at his big door patting his pockets and checking his bag. He can't find his key, I thought. He sighed and then bent down and reached into the back of one of the enormous plant pots standing each side of his door. He fished out a key and went inside. The shiny nameplate on the door flashed as he closed it.

Once I thought I saw him in the park with his family. I was killing time, just looking at the ducks, when this little boy flew by on a shiny scooter. A man I was sure was Mr. Behr jogged behind, calling encouragements. After him came a woman, laughing but with a nervous look in her eyes. She had glossy hair and the kind of jacket and boots that you see in the posters for ski holidays. It made me a bit sad. She reminded me of my mum. Not the clothes but just when she scooped the boy up and covered him in kisses. Mum used to do that. Before she got sick.

***

The door to the bedroom is opening and he's coming in. Mr. Behr and Mrs. Behr behind him. The little boy is further down the hall but I can see his frightened expression as he peers into his room.

"And they're still here!" Mr. Behr roars. His teeth are bared and there is spittle on his lips. I'm still sitting on the little low bed trying to get my legs to work to stand up and he looks enormous, standing over me, arms raised. Mrs. Behr shrieks.

"What the bloody hell are you…"

He stops dead.

"You!" he yells.

For a moment I think it's all going to be okay. But it isn't. He grabs me by the arm. I can feel last night's bruises smarting and as I rise, there is a screaming pain in my ribs. He marches me down the stairs past the boy and the woman whose look of fear has now morphed into disgust. I start to try and say something but he's shouting again, about chairs and chocolates and how dare I. He's twisting my arm behind my back with one hand and with the other he's taken out his mobile and I can see he's dialling 999.

We're in the hallway now and there's a load of suitcases and bags. His foot catches the strap of one and when his grip loosens, I take my chance and run. I'm out the door and off down Woodland Way before he knows what's up. I haven't shoplifted in years, but my legs still remember how to pump when they have to. They also know you don't have to do it for long if you can find a good place to hide. The back of a pub will do—all those barrels and outhouses and crates—to duck down for a while. Once the adrenalin has gone the pain comes back in my head and my ribs and my arm. I don't cry often—what's the point, you just look weak and no-one cares—but I do then. Big sobs of shame and sadness.

Crouching behind a pile of empty cardboard boxes, I think about the night before. What an idiot I'd been to have thought I'd be in any way welcome. I can see now how it must have looked. His wife was obviously terrified and the little boy… I didn't mean any harm and I certainly hadn't meant to fall asleep.

***

The cheap vodka from earlier and the whack to the head had made me a bit woozy. Kev had been in a worse rage than I'd ever seen him and for the first time I got properly frightened. I needed to get away and my mind was racing for where to go when I remembered the offer: *if I ever needed anything*. It was stupid but I thought I might just ring the bell and if nothing else at least Kev wouldn't do anything while I was stood at the door. The house was in darkness though and no-one answered. I was about to go when I remembered the key. I could slip inside for ten minutes until Kev had cooled down or passed out.

The hall was cold and dark. No alarm, I realised with surprise. I caught sight of myself in the hall mirror. My blonde hair was matted and dirty and there was blood streaking down my face from a cut just above my eye. A bruise was already coming out on my nose which looked a weird shape. *Sod you, Kev*, I thought angrily.

I was hungry and thirsty. The kitchen was a huge shining spaceship of white gloss and chrome at the back of the house looking onto the garden. The fridge was empty and the cupboards had nothing but some lentils with a funny name, those expensive coffee pods and a jar of olives. I looked round and saw three chocolate advent calendars propped up on the counter. I opened a door on the first one and stuffed the chocolate in my mouth. Yuck, dark chocolate. The next one looked better but I got a hard caramel and my jaw was hurting so I spat it out. The last calendar had pictures for kids and was full of little Christmas shapes in milk chocolate. I didn't even realise that I'd opened all the doors until I couldn't find another chocolate.

Suddenly, I felt dizzy and my head was aching so I sat down on a chair. It had one of those weird cushions on it for sore backs so I couldn't get comfy. The next chair was okay and I was settling in on the cushions when I saw the beanbag. I'd always wanted a beanbag as a kid. I got excited and sat down on it with a thump. My bum hit the floor and the little white beads went skittering all over the kitchen. *Shit*. I thought I'd better go then and headed back towards the front door. I needed a pee, I realised, and my eye was still dripping.

The big wide stairs with their soft cream carpet were right in front of me and I went up to look for a loo. The first room was about the size of the whole flat I grew up in. It had its own bathroom and I sorted myself out a bit. I suddenly felt very tired and I climbed onto the bed. It was covered in little shiny, slippery cushions which jumped about like fish. I couldn't relax with all that so I got up to look around a bit more. The next room was a sort of study with a desk and a big leather sofa covered with a throw like a polar bear fur. I touched it and it slid off the smooth leather and onto the floor with a soft *whump*. Startled, I ran out and into the next room. A boy's by the looks of the rockets and the Lego. Not that girls don't like these things of course. They do. I did—or did before toys became something that only other people had. The ceiling had those glow in the dark stars and someone had arranged them into proper constellations. It sounds stupid since I sleep outside a lot but right then all I wanted to do was to lie down on the bed and look up at them.

Fear at Forty-Three Thousand Feet by Yvonne Clarke

She looked into the mirror and saw a clown staring back at her. She couldn't apply her lipstick with a steady hand that morning; but flight crew were always expected to be meticulously turned out. As she wiped her lips and started again, she checked the crew list. Cabin supervisor Marcus, portly but competent—he always did this run if Julian was working the same rota. They weren't a couple, exactly, but she knew Marcus was working on it as he couldn't help telling anybody who would listen. Susie and Katie, both experienced cabin crew, happily married, their wild times in the world of long haul well over; Sven, Chris and Tim—relative newbies. Daisy and Alice in first class— they spoke in beautifully modulated voices, had the best figures and were ever so slightly sniffy about their status.

Kate peered into the mirror again. Her natural complexion was like porcelain—pale and unblemished, often admired, yet today her face had a ghostly pallor, despite the golden tan foundation and cheek tint. Her eyes, too, were red-rimmed and puffy, negating the effect of copious amounts of mascara. And her hair—so dull and lank. She sighed. How much longer could she keep up this charade?

Long ago, Kate had concluded that the glamour of working for an airline was overestimated. At the start of her career, the romance of world travel and a pool of young pilots to flirt with—possibly marry—had been irresistible. She used to gaze up at the vapour trails painting candy floss scars across the sky and dream. Not for her the nursing profession, nor working in a sick-syndrome office. She reflected on her naivety, recalling the fun she had had when training: learning how to do makeup and hair, the hilarity of the role-playing, and the evacuation procedure—down the slide, *go, go, go!* just like a child in a playground. No one focused on the tedium of doling out food and drink, collecting rubbish, mopping up vomit, pandering to inebriated passengers, calming down hysterical kids—and sometimes adults. And then there was the jet lag, which taunted your inner body clock relentlessly until you scarcely knew what day or time it was, or even which country you were in. Perhaps it was just as well her circumstances were about to change.

Briefing over, pre-flight procedures completed, time for boarding. Kate switched on her widest smile as the passengers approached in an accelerated walk which became a barely-disguised scrum as they fought to bag the best spots in the overhead lockers.

Then she saw him. A visceral wave of anticipation washed over her. He had turned right, not left. He *always* travelled First Class. Why would Mike be in Economy for this particular trip? Did he know she was on this flight? He thought it was all over. Instead, here she was, about to apply for maternity leave. She froze, barely breathing as he stretched out his six-foot-two self in seat H3.

"You alright, Kate?" Apart from being sharp-eyed, Marcus was a sensitive, empathetic soul. Someone you could confide in.

"Just a bit tired."

But she knew her attempt at deflection wouldn't fool him.

"I know there's something wrong, Kate. Spill the beans."

"Not here," she hissed, tilting her head towards the quieter rear end of the plane. She needed to undo the tangle of knitting in her mind.

Tears fogged her vision and left war-paint streaks of mascara on her cheeks. She rolled the words around inside her mouth before voicing them, abandoning chronology in favour of concision:

'...*molestation order... life together... baby... threats...*'.

Marcus's lower lip slipped south at Kate's revelation. Kate gave a percussive sniff, dabbed her eyes and reapplied a new-moon smile. She might be a prisoner at thirty thousand feet, but she had a job to do.

Back in the galley, she started to prepare the drinks trolley. Ding dong! Assistance requested, Seat H3.

"Will you go?" she asked one of the others.

"He's asking for you by name," came the response a minute later. "Nice looking guy—wouldn't turn *him* down."

Oh yes you would, thought Kate, if you knew him as well as I do.

"He can wait, I'm busy."

Several more G and T's later, Mike buzzed again. This time she was the only crew member free. His lanky frame was like that of a giraffe, long legs stretching out gawkily towards the emergency exit, a deliberately louche demeanour.

"Can I help you, Sir?"

He leaned towards her conspiratorially, his hostile glare scorching her retinas and his aphrodisiacal scent taking her back in time.

"Good to see you again Kate." His sloppy southern drawl was one of the things that had first attracted her to him.

She tried to modulate the timbre of her voice. "What can I get you?"

His chin jerked up like a puppet on a string. He had been waiting for this moment.

"What can *you* get *me*? Off the hook is what you can get me, bitch." His words cut into her heart as she attempted to maintain her composure. How she wished someone was sitting next to him—that would shut him up.

The sting of rejection fed her fighting spirit.

"We loved each other once. Did all our plans, all your promises, mean nothing to you? I'm having our baby, whatever you say, and you can be involved in its life or not. It's up to you."

His grimace morphed into a snarl, upper lip curling up on one side, like a cur about to attack. Muscles began to twitch in his lower jaw.

"I don't succumb to blackmail. You know that the Child Support Agency will be onto me as soon as you can say 'bastard', and if the tabloids sniff out the story, my reputation will be in tatters. I can kiss goodbye to winning a seat in any of the God-fearing southern states."

"Everything okay here?" It was Marcus.

"All in hand, thanks." She moved away.

"It's him, isn't it?"

"Yes. And he's had too much to drink."

"I'll keep an eye on him, don't worry." Marcus pirouetted gracefully one hundred and eighty degrees and walked off in the direction of the galley.

Kate reflected on her current situation. She had met Mike—good looking, successful, solvent—while doing a brief stint in First Class a year ago, and their attraction was mutual. Despite the fact that Mike was already married, they planned a future together one day. Then, as fast as a guillotine falls, the bond was cut. Their unborn child, conceived in love, had precipitated a maelstrom of hate. There was no question in his mind: the baby had to go. And he had flung a large wad of cash at her to enable the process—a process which she had no intention of following through.

But worse was to come. Mike had started stalking her. At first, she thought her mind was playing tricks, but as time went on she realised he was monitoring her closely. She changed the locks and kept her curtains drawn; she blocked his phone calls, but she was still on edge every time she left the house. He was issued with a molestation order, but it didn't stop the nightmares rattling round in her mind like a box of loose change. You cannot plot happiness or sorrow on a graph, she reasoned, but Mike had snuffed out her hopes as sure as the flat line on a heart monitor. Was she strong enough to follow this through alone?

Some time later, the passengers settled down for their pseudo-night time. But an unexpected smell—nicotine—started to waft through the cabin. As the smoke alarm sounded, Kate headed towards the source—a toilet in the middle of the plane. With some apprehension (you never knew how a passenger would react) she tapped lightly on the door. No answer. She tapped harder.

"Is anyone in there?" Silly question, but it had to be said. No answer.

"Open the door please." More authoritative now.

Suddenly the door folded back. She was grabbed firmly by the arm and dragged inside. Mike slammed the lock into place and leaned in towards her, jabbing his forefinger into her chest. She recoiled at the noxious odours of alcohol and cigarette breath as they punched her in the face.

"No one messes with me, understand? You're going to pay for this!" A string of saliva escaped from the corner of his mouth. Kate could almost hear the churning of nausea in her belly. She froze like a captured animal, an instinctive survival mechanism.

Mike flexed his fingers theatrically before delicately teasing open the buttons on her blouse and loosening his belt with a lascivious leer.

"Get off me!" she yelled, hoping to alert the nearby passengers. He clamped one hand over her mouth and she felt the washbasin unit digging into her back as he pushed her hard against it. The ash from his cigarette, like the fake snow in a snow globe, fell in drifts onto her jacket.

Desperation, however, had sharpened her wits: if she could kick sideways on the locked door with the tip of her right foot, she had a chance. As he wrestled to restrain her, he hesitated for a nanosecond, and her strategy paid off. Mike was led away in handcuffs, weaving an inebriated path along the aisle, all the while yelling a flowing torrent of abuse.

Back in the crew's quarters, cocooned in the warmth of a blanket and sipping a cup of hot, sweet tea, Kate closed her eyes and succumbed to the solicitous ministrations of Marcus. What a star. She would ask him to be the godfather of her child.

When they landed, the airport police led Mike away. It turned out that he already had a string of GBH convictions. He wouldn't be flying with Kate's airline ever again.

Meanwhile, Hong Kong, one of her favourite destinations, was beckoning. The ride to Victoria Peak, the cacophony of the ubiquitous Star ferries, the retail mecca of

Kowloon. Three glorious days to recuperate, then back home to start her new life on *terra firma*.

The Chair by Miki Lentin

Jerry sat on the toilet listening to BBC Radio Five Live. He was holding the 'guidance for patients' leaflet on photocopied, stapled white A4 sheets of paper. Lucy, his wife, had told him nonchalantly that she'd found a lump in her left breast while they were watching TV on the sofa.

"So, I found a lump in my breast," she said.

"Oh?" Jerry responded.

"Yeah, I'm not going to worry about it, but I've made an appointment to see the Consultant. Tomorrow."

"Which one?"

"The left one."

Jerry went to go and feel it, but she shook him away.

"I just want to see what it feels like," Jerry said.

Jerry read the leaflet about breast cancer. He repeated the words he read quietly to himself. Breast, cancer, surgery, radiotherapy, diagnosis, consultation, support, charity, family. He'd taken it off the kitchen counter so the kids wouldn't see it. She said he could read up about it, get informed. Jerry didn't really know what that meant, but in between the anthems playing at the start of a World Cup match, he tried his best to study the leaflet. He folded it and stuffed it into the pocket of his combat shorts, next to the other white photocopied letter he'd received that day.

***

The waiting room was busy the next morning. Jerry and Lucy waited patiently for her appointment. She played with her mobile and Jerry sat in his grey suit, which felt a bit tight around his thighs, and looked around at the others waiting, mostly women. A trolley of tea and coffee was being served by two elderly volunteers in blue bibs who struggled to pick up the old metal teapot with a long spout that poured scalding water into Styrofoam cups.

"Tea, coffee?" one of the volunteers cheerily asked, manoeuvring the trolley closer to Jerry.

"No thank you," he replied.

"You sure love? Looks like you need one."

"I'm fine, thank you."

Jerry looked up over his glasses at the telly. *Antiques Roadshow* was on repeat and the presenters were burbling loudly about an old looking porcelain vase with what looked like sea urchins stuck to the outside. *Is that what a lump looks like?* Jerry thought.

"Lucy Ryan," an elderly Consultant, wearing a frayed blue tie tucked into his white shirt called.

Lucy put her long black hair into a ponytail, grabbed her puffer coat and disappeared behind door number four. Jerry held her hand tightly before she left, letting go at just the last second. She smiled at him.

"Nothing to worry about," she said.

Jerry knew that if the appointment was more than five minutes he'd worry. A bit like having to hold a one nil lead for the last five minutes of a football game he thought. If you were able to take the ball into the corner and hold it there, mess around, he liked to call it, then you'd sap the opposition's energy and territory. That was only possible for five minutes, so he knew if the appointment went over five minutes, he could start to worry.

Jerry hadn't told Lucy about his job at the charity. The

Head of Department and an HR Business Partner had called him into the windowless 'HR Confidential Room' the previous day at lunch time, when the rest of the office was quiet. They had asked him to take a seat. He'd sat down, noticing that the soft purple cushion of the chair was warm, as if someone else had recently vacated it, and that the box of tissues on the table was empty.

They had smiled at him, looking up from their laptops every few sentences. They'd told him that they were making cut-backs and restructures across the organisation, and his role would no longer exist. As they had spoken Jerry's mind had began to wander, and he'd looked at the large screen TV bracketed onto the wall, and had thought of ways that he could have stolen it, as it was a far superior model to his telly. They had given him a document with details of his severance, his duties while on gardening leave, and information about the free confidential counselling service, should he want it. They'd asked if he wanted to call someone. He'd thought for a moment and had said, "no, thank you". Jerry had got up from the chair and had carefully pushed it under the table.

"Jerry?" Lucy said, "Jerry?"

He looked up startled.

"I have to go for a mammogram and an MRI."

"What did he say?"

"He had a feel and thinks it's nothing, thank goodness, but just in case, you know, they want to see inside."

Jerry pictured the Consultant routinely examining his wife's left breast. Jerry thought that he'd love to see a photo of what it looked like inside. He enjoyed looking at photos of the human body in science books and seeing how it was made up of tissue, water, blood vessels and sinew all looped together in beautiful knots.

They sat outside another room in a low-ceilinged corridor lit by humming strip lights. There was no tea or coffee or telly to watch, so Jerry ran his finger over the letter in his pocket, checked his emails and thought about how he'd tell Lucy. What would they say to the kids? Who would they tell? How would he deal with it? How would he tell the lads? Would he gather them around in the pub and just tell them that he'd lost his job and his wife had cancer? Would they feel sorry for him when he went for a piss at half-time and tone down their voices when he returned? Would it be the same, with her, with them, with anyone?

Lucy was called into a room with a yellow radioactive sign above the door, like some nuclear reactor. A skinny woman with shoulder length black hair walked down the corridor and sat next to Jerry.

"Mmm, excuse me, my wife is sitting there, she'll be out in a minute," Jerry said, and looked up at the woman, noticing that she was biting her raw fingernails.

"Oh," she said, "but I was told to sit here by the Consultant, so I'd get noticed."

"There are some other chairs over there," Jerry said, pointing at them.

The woman didn't move for a few minutes. Jerry's foot lightly brushed her brown leather boot, so he folded his legs the other way. She sighed heavily, stood up and sat in a chair on the other side of the corridor.

Jerry thought of the purple chairs in the 'HR Confidential Room', and how many people must have sat on them over the past few days listening to bad news, and slowly emptying the box of tissues.

"Oh, don't sit there," the first woman said to a new

arrival who went to sit next to Jerry, "you don't want to sit next to that gentleman!" she said mockingly.

"There are other free chairs over there," Jerry said, "I'm holding this one for my wife. She'll be out in a minute."

"I bloody hate people like that," the first woman said loudly to her new chair neighbour while staring at Jerry. "People who think they own the place, self-righteous twats," she continued.

Her neighbour nodded and squinted at Jerry with her small eyes and crinkly face.

The door to the reactor opened, but it was only a nurse in green overalls and a hair net. She smiled generously at those waiting as her rubber shoes squeaked along the shiny corridor. Jerry all of a sudden felt very alone. He couldn't get the words cancer or counselling out of his head. He wanted to feel the outside and see the inside for himself, to make sure they got it right, but what did he know? He'd only read the information leaflet. He was only the man with no job. All the words of the past two days poured back to him: breast, cancer, surgery, restructure, radiotherapy, gardening, diagnosis, consultation, support, charity, family, severance, counselling, confidential, chair.

A mobile phone rang. The first woman answered it.

"Hello? Look, I can't talk now—I'm having a, a check-up. Yeah. Yeah... oh, the hospital. They found something. You know, a lump thingy. In my breast. Fuckin' hurts. Yeh, look I can't talk now. I'll give you a call later, alright? Alright, I'll talk to you later," she said through quiet sobs.

The door opened again and those waiting looked up. Lucy sat down.

"Well?" Jerry asked.

"They don't think it's anything."

"That's good. Did they see what's inside?"

"They clamped my breast with two metal plates and took some x-rays. I have to go back upstairs. It's nothing, you can go to work now."

"No, no, I'll stay with you," Jerry held her hand.

As Cold as a Winter's Day by Derek Hulme

"Colonel Mustard did it in the library with the candlestick," I make the accusation, letting Mrs. White the cook rattle down onto the board. My two sons, Timothy and Stephen, let out a groan in unison and Lucy, my youngest, sighs.

However, Helen tries to raise their hopes. "Come on let's see if your father is right first, before we get too despondent. You should know by now he will take a chance and declare early if he thinks anyone else is getting close."

My wife is right. She knows me well. We met on the first day at high school and she was the only girl I could talk to for the first couple of years. She wasn't like the other girls. You could hold a normal conversation with her, and she would join in the playground games, while the other girls stood around the edges smirking. Not that I saw her as a mate. Don't make that mistake. I always wanted more than that. I knew we would be the perfect couple and there was only that one time I had any doubts. I smile at her and she smiles back knowingly. Her eyes crease in the corners, in that way that melts me. Yes, she knows me well because I am definite it is Colonel Mustard and positive it is the library, but I'm not sure about the candlestick; there is a chance it is the dagger. However, why wait until next go and watch Timothy or Stephen get lucky and pip me at the post?

I slip the cards from the black envelope and the candlestick is on top. I have found it always pays to play the odds. Not recklessly when the odds are against you, but if the odds are in your favour you have to take your chances in life. Grasp the opportunity when it comes along. 'Faint heart never won…' That attitude made me so successful on the racing track and then later, on the stock market. It has brought me a lovely, comfortable life. We're not stinking rich, two or three million if you include all the assets, not like Nelson's father. He had been obscenely rich; Nelson had owned a couple of motorbikes when he started high school and had a small fleet before the end.

Helen's telling 'the story' again. "Your father was always the bravest person I knew. You should have seen how his body brushed the track when he broadsided into the curve to overtake on a bend. Then there was the time he risked his life trying to save a friend of mine. Got in the papers and everything. The lad's father was so grateful that he rewarded him, you know." The brothers shoot a look at each other. They do know. They've heard this story quite a few times before. Lucy is listening, she is proud of her old dad and doesn't yet have any of her brothers' anxieties about living up to the example I have set.

Helen has the newspaper cuttings somewhere, but for me it wasn't the short-lived celebrity that was important. Nelson's father rewarded me with a couple of his lad's motorbikes and a fair amount of money. It was my lucky break. The bikes and the money set me up in the sport and set me on track to fame and fortune.

As I sit down in my armchair sipping a glass of a twenty-five year old Glenfarclas, I glance out the window and notice the snow is falling quite heavily. It is very reminiscent of that winter's afternoon. I would have been a few years older than Timothy is now, around fifteen or sixteen. It was December, so before my birthday, so I would have been fifteen. Something was on my mind that afternoon and I couldn't settle in the house. So, despite the heavy snow, I jogged down to the local park and took my frustrations out on my new football. In less than a quarter of an hour, the ball had rolled down the path and out onto the frozen lake. I wasn't going to leave it there, so I crawled out onto the ice to retrieve it. I had just managed to get a hand on it when the ice started creaking in a most alarming way. I couldn't risk turning round and crawled backwards off the lake. If I had ventured any further out onto the lake... On the bank was a stout branch. I remember thinking *if I had fallen in, someone might have pulled me out with that.* I looked around but there was no one in the park. That's when I decided to call on Nelson.

I persuaded Nelson to bring his new skateboard and we took turns riding it down the icy path. When I fell off, I gave it a good kick and sent it out onto the lake. Nelson was livid and only half believed me when I blamed my fall on a wild animal running across the path. Of course, he couldn't see the white rabbit I pointed out to him on the snowy bank. Neither could I. He wanted me to get the skateboard back for him, but I told him I was too scared after nearly falling in retrieving my ball. He laughed and said anything I could do he could do. I knew he would say that. I made a good pretense of rescuing him with the branch in case anyone should arrive on the scene, while making sure he went under the ice.

Helen grieved for a time because Nelson had been making a bit of a play for her and I had noticed she was interested. I don't blame her. All that money must have been tempting. I made a good job of comforting her and it all turned out as I had hoped in the end—better than I had hoped with the reward from his father—I am not a murderer, not really. I didn't enjoy it or anything like that. I have not killed anyone else since. But you have to take your chances in life, don't you?

The Displacement Artist by David DeWinter

Another drive home after the deed is done.

I say deed, it's just my job. A little earner on the side.

It is what I am paid to do so it is not an act of my choosing as such, just a necessary dirty job and as the old cliché goes, someone has to do it. That someone is me.

When I pull the switch, when I send those currents coursing through their body until dead, I maintain a calm steady easiness. It's called being a professional.

The first time I flipped the switch for some delinquent murderous psychopath, well that was hard I must admit. Real hard. But then I thought why should he get a pardon or an easy ride in some cosy, cute prison? No sir, that son-of-a-bitch broke into a convenience store and blew away a young college kid working behind the counter before turning the gun on three customers. He killed two and crippled the other.

So uh, excuse me if I don't shit it over that evil monster. Once it was over, the rest came easy. Logic kicked in you see? These sickos deserve it.

I can't go around killing people like that, indiscriminately. Hell, I even worried for that first guy when he merited nothing. What a fool I was.

Anyway, today was my twenty second execution and it was as uneventful as the others. Apart from the paintings.

Nice and easy, job done, while inside of me a cold calm takes over.

That has been the way. I can retreat into my own sanity while the latest mad dog squirms and jives in the chair; then nothing. Some of them used to try screaming for mercy or sympathy, a last moment reprieve while others did nothing. It made little difference to me.

A former friend of mine, Todd, he went all fancy on me, he said that some of these so called people have mental health problems. Talked of all sorts, multiple personalities and 'schizosomething,' I don't know.

Sounded like a load of pampering horse shit to me and it didn't save those victims did it? No sir. They are dead and then people like my former buddy have the cheek to say, 'Eww, let's look after em, let's study them so we can see the why and what for.'

Waste of time.

We drifted after that conversation. He found himself a woman, had himself a son and daughter. I told him straight when visiting them one day, 'Them kid's best not ask to sit on my lap, I ain't having that wife of yours shouting ooh wee look he's a goddamn child fiddler!'

That's the way of the world now. A man like me, hard working all his damned life, never harmed no one who didn't deserve it, can be accused of all sorts while murderous freaks deserve our understanding and time? I can tell you who sounds crazy based on that.

Well, now it's just me and I'm fine with it. The more time I spend with people, the further out I feel. I used to have a beer with Todd a few nights each week, he'd come on over to the trailer and we'd laugh about them good ole days. We both started off in construction and we had a colourful life, let me put it that way. We could handle ourselves in any bar room brawl and we mixed it with the best of them.

But, that as I say, that was before Todd got all educated on me or got to thinking, as he was fond of saying. 'Oh hey, Randall, I got to thinking,' he'd say before coming out with some new age bullshit or spewing some science jargon.

He got to lecturing me about the death penalty, all these findings, talking about people with head injuries and traumas effecting their behaviour. Of kids who didn't know no better and needed proper help. How we should help em and learn some, not execute them. He pleaded almost. Won't you help them? Think about it, please?

But I was so angry on the inside that I just switched him off. When I couldn't turn him off, when his words started getting through somehow, well instead of killing the son-of-a-bitch for the insults and downright impoliteness of lecturing me in my own trailer, I broke contact. Told him in so many words where to go.

I used to miss him on the nights after an execution, when we just chewed the shit and laughed about whatever. It was a nice distraction in a way, not that I needed it mind you for I was at peace, you understand.

So recently, after my work is done on nights like tonight, I get home and have me a few beers and smokes… then I get to painting. Strangest thing, I don't actually remember the painting part but the colour filled canvas is there in the morning alright. I have me quite the collection now.

It's like I switch off altogether, don't think a goddamned thing. I've no idea if the paintings are any good, I don't much care really. They give me something and that is what counts, although, I've no idea what.

It's called displacement behaviour, Randall.

You leave me be Todd!

Some friend, not content enough to ruin our friendship he's also left some of himself in my head. He's not the only one in there digging around neither. Todd will be quiet once I get in and set up for painting.

Only slight problem I have these days, is these paintings of mine sort of scare me some. Sounds silly I know but when I first started painting them, I barely cared or looked at them. Not for long anyways. Just a glance for a short while then I'd tuck them under the bed. But not anymore. Now I get up in the morning and stare at them for ages. They looked other worldly to me and this morning, before driving off, I put them altogether and they seem to make a bigger picture.

Made me nervous looking at it for a while before I put them from my mind and had me a liquid breakfast.

They are coming for you, Randall.

Shut up, Todd!

I should have buried you at birth.

I don't like that voice. Daddy was a bad man, he may have killed Ma. I can't be sure, I just used to hear scraping from the basement or her 'special place,' and Daddy used to smile, especially when I told him the scraping had stopped one day.

I pull up in the park, everyone is sleeping or passed out. None of them aware of the work I've done this night. It is challenging to be an unsung hero.

I get inside and grab me my beers, time to get through

the twelve pack and see what comes out on canvas tonight. When I put them all together this morning, those paintings, and I don't wish to dwell on this too long, but all the dark swirls and smudged blood finger prints, the blossoming explosions and black wavering lines, they all made sense.

The paintings cover the entire side of the wall.

As I stare at them now, paint at the ready and as the beer softens my anxieties, those swirls almost dance in front of me.

Let's paint me some more, Randall.

I always hear that layered voice before I lose myself and...

My word, where are my manners. I fell away again.

I warned you, once the painting starts I just about disappear. My head bang's like a drum. What did I produce last night I wonder?

I don't have to look far, its right up there on the wall with the others, and boy it completes the picture alright. There they are, the dead ones, those I killed in the name of law and justice. I know it is them because of the sound they make.

On my wall, looms a large bent head and face with enormous fluid charcoal eyes and an eternal mouth. Its stretching as I tell you of this, that mouth is a hole leading to somewhere just awful. I can smell that place from my trailer and it is wrong.

I burn the lot. Trash, nasty trash. Think I'm going to drink some more once this headache passes. It's a doozy, like someone crammed my heart into my skull.

Maybe the thing on the wall did just that.

Todd again. He won't shut up.

You'd have to have a heart to begin with I guess.

Damn him, I'm going for a walk. The woods, the air is clear there and free of noise... and of Todd. I feel better already, the banging in my temples is easing and I'm starting to feel fresh. No more bullshit voices. Sat here deep among the trees, I feel peace.

A twig snaps somewhere behind and wakes me.

I know it's no animal. I can tell because of the way my skin feels. Swallowing seems real hard and the woods are too dark as I turn around to see what lurks.

It's the thing from my painting, the way it moves brings on nausea. It shifts on legs that must be broken or deformed, dragging soundlessly along the forest floor in awkward yet precise movements. It tilts that insanely long head to the side, staring at me.

I stare right back.

You need to run, Randall. This ain't no displacement episode. That thing is real.

Todd! I'll stay right where I am, you know nothing. Never did, you snowflake.

The thing shifts around me, closing the space as it

circles. The air crackles with an electricity, coming up from the ground beneath me in pulses. I can feel the vibrations.

Maybe you'll see Mama again, Randall, and Daddy is going to be along in no time at all.

You stay out of this Pa!

The head remains tilted as it gets closer. Too close. I see the giant holes where eyes should be while that mouth, that gaping horrendous mouth is filled with swirling rows of teeth. Only, its teeth are needles, endless rows of them chomping down and releasing some sort of solution in amidst its own blood filled lacerations.

I'm screaming. The space between us closed and it is upon me, the pit of my stomach is wrenched in terror.

I don't want to die alone out here. This thing will open me up.

Won't you help me?

Please?

Thank you for reading our first anthology.

If you would like to enter a piece of writing or find out more about what we do, please visit our website for more information:

www.glitteryliterary.com

Printed in Great Britain
by Amazon